KOLO AND
THE MIGHTY
MANGOES

KOLO AND THE MIGHTY MANGOES

DAVE CASWELL

ISBN, paperback: 978-1-80227-113-3
ISBN, ebook: 978-1-80227-114-0

This book is typeset in New Caledonia LT Std

"Kolo and the Mighty Mangoes is a brilliantly engaging story that will not only capture the minds of its readers, but also teach valuable life lessons. The questions at the end of each chapter help the reader to examine their own decision making and behaviour, and ultimately provide a great way for them to develop positive character building. The story is great for individuals to read on their own but also perfect for children's book clubs, football teams, and other groups where the readers can read, discuss and learn together."

- Simon Thomas (Sports Presenter, Author and Podcaster)

"A great story run through with so many vital moments of learning that will definitely help children to focus on who they are and who they are becoming. And yes - It may well have been written for young readers but Kolo and the Mighty Mangoes is a story that can help all of us to think about all those 'vital moments' we have every day where we get to choose what kind of person we want to be."

- Jill Rowe (Ethos & Formation Director, Oasis UK)

"An amazing story about football and being a better person. I learnt about working together with your friends, about forgiving others, and about telling the truth."

- Lucas, aged 10.

DEDICATION

To Mom and Dad.

CONTENTS

ACKNOWLEDGEMENTS

Thanks to everyone at Publishing Push for your help, support and expertise in bringing this story to print.

To all my friends and colleagues at Oasis who are a constant source of support and inspiration, thanks for who you are and all you do. Special thanks to Jill Rowe and Michelle Briers for your specific input and encouragement on this project.

Thanks to Simon Thomas for your review and endorsement.

Big thanks to all those who have supported me and my work with Oasis over the years. You are very much appreciated. Special thanks to Clive Gordon, Gavin Shepherd, Stuart Jones, and Jonathon Gordon, who have supported me from day one and continue to give their time and energy in helping me do what I do.

To my amazing family: you are a continuous source of love, laughter and encouragement. Thanks for supporting me every step of the way.

Finally, thanks to the Oasis Football for Life family around the world. Your dedication, sacrifice, and heart for community is a daily inspiration. Together we are shaping the future.

INTRODUCING KOLO

These stories were primarily written as part of the "Oasis Football for Life & Oasis 9 Habits Training Manual" – a resource for use in Oasis Football for Life programmes.

Stories can often help children and young people understand moral or ethical issues much better than simply being taught about them in a formal education setting. This is especially true in cultures that have an oral and storytelling tradition and where moral tales and storytelling are part of the culture and context.

These stories centre around a young boy called Kolo. Kolo is the central focus of the stories, and children are encouraged, through the stories, to put themselves in the position of Kolo and discuss how they would feel and react. They may already have found themselves in such situations before, but discussing them in a group or team setting can help find answers to difficult situations and help them make wise and healthy life choices going forward.

In the first story, Kolo arrives in a new village with his mother and young sister. From then on, he faces different situations and challenges as he settles, makes friends and encounters many of the challenge's children (and adults) face in their own lives.

Each story has a focus on a particular habit or life skill, with questions at the end for thought and discussion, but there are also many other related habits and life skills woven into each story.

Enjoy.

Dave Caswell

Chapter 1

KOLO'S FOOTBALL

The hot sun shone down on Kolo's head as he bounced and jerked along with the movements of the truck. He was sat in the back with his younger sister, Suri. They were moving from their old house to a new one in a new village, and their job was to make sure all the family's furniture and belongings were safe.

He dug his hand down into the bag of clothes that he had strategically placed to use as a seat. His sister was small enough to sit in a washing basin, safely wedged between a cupboard and a chair, and was quite content there, watching the world go by.

Reaching into the bottom of the bag, Kolo found what he was looking for. It was one of his old schoolbooks, which he knew he could use as a hat, or at least as a cover, to protect his head from the hot sun. Why they had chosen to travel during the hottest time of the day was a mystery to him, but Kolo was nothing if not creative, and he knew if he folded the book in a certain way, it would make a nice hat, and he could fit it perfectly to rest around his ears.

As he tried to pull the book from the bottom of the bag (it was a very tightly packed bag, and Kolo wondered if his mum had put everything in the world in there), the back of his hand felt something else, something smooth, something round – it was his football!

Kolo loved football; any chance he got to play, he would – before school, after school, at weekends, even in the garden when he was supposed to be digging and weeding, or when he went to fetch water from the borehole! Carrying a big jerrycan of water while dribbling his football was quite a difficult task, but Kolo always saw it as good training – although he didn't think anyone had ever played a whole football match while carrying a jerrycan!

Kolo had played football in a team where they used to live, but now they were moving, he had had to say goodbye to the team and all his friends. It had been a very sad day. He didn't understand why they had to move, and it was not his decision, but Kolo knew he had to respect his mother, even if he did have to leave all his friends behind. He hoped he would make new friends when they reached their new home - and join a new team!

Kolo's mother was very kind and understood how hard it was for him to leave. It's always hard and always sad to say goodbye to those you care about, but Kolo's mother had told him to be hopeful that new friends, a new life, and maybe even a new team would lie ahead.

Because she was kind and because she was compassionate, Kolo's mum had done a very nice thing. On that very morning, the day they were leaving, she had called Kolo in from outside where he was helping to pack the truck. She led him into the main room in the house and sat him down (it was actually the *only* room in the house, apart from the kitchen).

"Now, Kolo," she said, "I know it is hard for you to leave, and I know you will miss your friends, but I've got you a little present to make you feel a little bit happier."

With that, she twisted her body round to the back of the chair she was sitting on (and which was one of the few things left in the house) and turned back with a brand-new football in her hands!

"I hope this can make you feel a bit less sad," she said.

"Oh, thank you, mum! Thank you so much!" yelled Kolo.

He shouted so loud in fact that his sister ran into the house, and even a passing goat stuck its head in the door to see what all the commotion was about. The chickens in the compound just scattered in different directions. Chickens are not very brave, and it is a known fact that they don't like footballs.

Kolo was extremely grateful, especially as he knew his mother didn't have a lot of money and must have sacrificed things to buy the football. He gave her a big hug. So big, in fact, that he feared he might squeeze all the goodness out of her. Thankfully for her, the truck driver bibbed the horn, and it was time to go.

"Now," said Kolo's mother, "make sure you look after that football. Put it in the bottom of the bag with all the clothes in and keep it safe."

Kolo had done what he was told (though it was a squeeze to get it in). He knew it would be safe in there – and to make it extra safe, that was one of the reasons he sat on the bag in the back of the truck.

Anyway, here he was, in the truck, and as he felt the ball against his hand, he instantly forgot about the old schoolbook and the hot sun on his head.

'Surely it won't hurt to hold the ball for a while?' he thought.

Kolo pushed his hand deeper between the side of the bag and the football and managed to cup his hand under the bottom of the ball (if balls even have a bottom?). He pulled and pulled, rolling the ball up the inside of the bag. Further and further it moved, until eventually, with Kolo at this point sweating from all his effort, it shot out of the top of the bag and into the air. The bag had been so tightly packed with clothes that a t-shirt and three socks also came out with it!

Kolo put the t-shirt and socks back into the bag and sat with the ball in his lap. He had never had his own football before. It was brand new, perfectly round and smooth, and shining in the midday sun.

Kolo sat there for a while, just holding the ball and dreaming of playing and scoring the winning goal in the cup final. Almost without thinking, he began bouncing the ball off his knees, first one knee, then the other, and then one to the other and back again as he got more and more confident. He knew the day was going to turn out to be a good one.

Then suddenly, the truck went over a particularly large bump and did the biggest bounce of the entire journey.

Kolo bounced up in the air, his sister Suri and the washing basin she was sitting in bounced up in the air together (as if the basin was part of her body) and back down into its original position, and Kolo's new ball bounced off his knees, off a saucepan, and off the truck!

Kolo could barely speak. His heart sank so much that he felt, if he didn't have toes, it would have dropped right out of his feet. His ball, the ball his mother had been so kind to buy for him, bounced down the dirt track at full speed, with the truck moving further and further away in the opposite direction. Kolo watched as the ball bounced off a tree, changed direction slightly, and rolled off into a bushy area at the side of the road.

Moments later, a small boy wearing a white t-shirt with a picture of a mango on it walked out of the bushy area holding the football and looking at the truck as it disappeared into the distance.

"My football, my football!" shouted Kolo as loud as he could. Thankfully, however, it was not so loud that his mother could hear over the noise of the truck's engine and the fact she was sat with the driver in the cabin. The truck turned a corner and came to a stop.

"We're here!" shouted Kolo's mother.

Kolo leapt off the truck and ran back along the track they had just driven down. It was not that far from where his football had bounced off.

"I'll be back soon," he shouted back to his mum. "I'll help unpack when I come back."

Kolo's younger sister looked at her odd brother and wondered, as much as any 6-year-old ever wonders, if she was actually stuck in the washing basin.

Compassionate & Considerate

1. What did you think of the story?

2. How was Kolo's mum compassionate and considerate?

3. How would you feel if you were Kolo?

4. Have you ever been in a situation like this?

   a. How did you feel?

   b. What did you do?

   c. What was the outcome?

5. What would you do if you were the boy who found Kolo's football?

6. Are there things we can learn from the story?

7. What should Kolo do next?

Kolo and the Mighty Mangoes

Chapter 2

KOLO AND MIDI

Kolo ran and ran. He knew where his football had bounced off the truck. He could remember the giant mango tree with the branches that hung across the road and where the boy had appeared holding his ball. It was the last thing he had seen before the truck had turned the corner and stopped at their new home. He just had to follow the road, and in truth, it wasn't that far from the mango tree.

He reached the mango tree, gasping for breath. It wasn't a long distance, but Kolo had run so fast - almost as fast as that time Mrs Nata had chased him when he'd accidentally knocked over her saucepan with a football.

His heart was pumping fast, and deep in the pit of his stomach, he felt a mixture of worry and shame – a twisting and turning motion, like the one his mother made when preparing beans.

He looked all around him.

'It must be around here somewhere,' he thought. 'That boy must be around here somewhere!'

He looked and looked, but there was nothing and no one around. He could only see a group of cows grazing in a field just down from the mango tree, and he knew *they* couldn't have taken his football. For a slight moment, he wondered if they might have eaten it – he knew that cows liked to eat, and he'd even heard that they had four stomachs, but no, his football had gone.

He sat down with his back against the large mango tree and cried. He had been so stupid, and he had let his mother down badly. She had been so kind to him, and he had not listened to her about keeping the football safe. He had even run away when he was supposed to be helping unload the truck, and he knew he'd also be in trouble for that.

"Oh God," he cried through his tears, "I'm so sorry. Please help me find my football..."

Just then, something very strange happened. Kolo's football dropped from the sky and into his lap!

Kolo didn't quite know what to do. He was, of course, very excited and very happy to see his football again, but had God really given him back his football?

He looked up towards the sky but could only see the thick green leaves of the mango tree. It was very old and very big and had big ripe mangoes everywhere.

But there was also something else. Through the leaves and the mangoes, Kolo spotted a glimpse of something white. Then he saw more of it, and then more. It seemed to be moving along one of the biggest branches, and it was making a noise. The noise sounded like a strange mixture of an animal grunting, someone trying to blow their nose very quietly, and the sound of a soda bottle when you open it.

Then the noise changed from all the odd sounds Kolo was imagining (he had a very good imagination) to a very recognisable one – laughter.

And then Kolo saw him. It was the boy in the white t-shirt he had seen earlier from the back of the truck.

"Hello," the boy shouted down to Kolo, who was now more confused than ever. "Sorry for laughing," he continued, "but you have to admit it is quite funny. My name's Midi. Wait there; I'm coming down."

Kolo agreed it was quite funny, and he was extremely relieved that he had got his football back - however it might have happened.

Midi made his way down the mango tree (he was obviously an expert at climbing trees) and sat down next to Kolo.

Kolo introduced himself and shared that he had just moved to the village.

"Thanks for giving me my football back," he said to Midi.

"That's okay. I know what it's like to lose something important or to have someone steal your things, and I could see how upset you were."

"It was funny," said Kolo, "I prayed to God to give me my ball back and then it fell from the sky!"

The boys laughed, and Kolo again thanked Midi for being so kind.

"You do know I'm not God, don't you?" said Midi, and the boys laughed again. "…But I think helping each other and being kind is what God probably wants us to do, so in a way, I was trying to be like him, even though I'm not him!" he continued.

It was not long before the two boys started talking about football. Kolo explained how much he loved the game and that he was a striker in his old team before he had to leave.

"It's too bad that I had to leave. I'll miss my old team, and it makes me feel so sad that I'll never play with them again," he said.

"Yes, that is tough," Midi said, "but you should try to stay positive and even happy if you can. We all face difficult things. Don't give up hope that you will play football in a team again. Look what just happened; you thought you'd lost your football, and then from nowhere, well, from a mango tree to be precise, things changed! Always have hope, Kolo."

"Wow!" said Kolo, "I wish I could be like you. I get so upset and frustrated at times."

"It just takes practice - and having good friends to help you," Midi replied. "Which reminds me, what are you doing on Saturday?"

"I don't think I'm doing anything," said Kolo. "I don't know anything or anyone here yet - apart from you."

"Meet me here, at this mango tree, at 7 am – and bring your football," Midi said and then ran off, waving back at Kolo as he shot through some bushes and out of sight.

Kolo walked back to where his new house was, and which was easy to find. He just had to follow the road, and in truth, it wasn't that far from the giant mango tree. When he reached there, his mother had just finished unloading all their belongings and was talking to the driver, probably about payment for the truck hire.

Kolo quickly sneaked around the side of the truck to where the bag of clothes had been placed and managed to squeeze his football back in the bag as if it had never been removed in the first place. He'd only just finished when his mother turned around.

"There you are!" she exclaimed, "Where have you been? Running off like that without any good cause and leaving me and the driver to do all the unloading!"

She wasn't happy. But it *was* for a 'good cause' Kolo thought to himself, I had to rescue my football!!! (But of course, he didn't say this. Some things are best not said.)

"I'm sorry, I had to.... er... I saw... I thought... I thought we had dropped one of the cooking pots off the back of the truck, and I went to get it," he lied, not very well.

"Well, where is it?" his mother asked. Clearly, Kolo was not holding a cooking pot.

"I made a mistake," said Kolo, "nothing had actually fallen off," he lied again.

"Okay then, but you can't just disappear like that without telling me, especially in a new place where we don't know anybody yet," his mother said, not totally convinced by Kolo's story.

Kolo knew that it wasn't exactly true that they didn't know anybody, he at least had met someone, and Midi had given him some good advice about being positive, joyful and hopeful that situations can change.

"You know, mum," he said, "I think things are going to be good here; you just need to stay joyful and hopeful, even when things are a bit tough."

"Is that so?" his mother said smiling. "Now, help me with your sister. She's refusing to get out of the washing basin."

Joyful & Hopeful

1. What did you like about the story? What things 'stuck out' for you?

2. Did you like Midi? What did you like about him?

3. Why do you think Kolo lied to his mother about why he had run back along the road?

4. Have you ever experienced anything similar to what happened in the story?

5. What did you think about Midi's advice to Kolo?

6. Why do you think Midi wanted to meet with Kolo on Saturday?

Kolo and the Mighty Mangoes

Chapter 3

KOLO MEETS THE MANGOES

The next day, Kolo and his family got settled into their new home.

There were many people staying in the houses around them, but they all seemed nice enough. There was the family in the opposite house who had 6 or 7, or maybe even 8 children; Kolo couldn't keep count of them all, and they were always running around, which made it even harder to count! One of the girls was about the same age as Kolo's sister, and they had become almost instant friends. As well as both being girls and of similar age, they both liked sitting in washing basins.

Then there was a man and his wife who also lived opposite but to the other side. She had big curly hair, and the man rode a bicycle.

Directly next to Kolo's house lived an old man, who Kolo learnt was called Wilbur. Old Man Wilbur would sit on a stool outside his house for what seemed like the whole day. When they had first arrived, he was there, and when Kolo had woken up the next morning and gone outside to wash his face, he was there again. Kolo wondered if, when Wilbur was young, someone had put glue on the stool, and he had just been stuck there ever since, just getting older.

Old Man Wilbur was thin with a bald head and with white whiskers all over his chin. He was also very friendly and was always waving at people passing by. Lots of people would stop and talk with him, and he never seemed annoyed like some old people Kolo knew. One of the most striking things about Old Man Wilbur, though, was that he was always laughing.

Kolo's mother had got a job in the local bakery but wasn't due to start for a few days. Kolo had got a place at the local school, but as it was the school holidays, he also didn't start for another week, so they both had time to settle into their new home.

Kolo spent the day helping his mother to clean and organise the house. He worked very hard and was very tired by the end of the day.

The next day was Saturday, the day he was supposed to meet Midi at the large mango tree, and he woke up early, as soon as the sun had also woken up and shot sunlight through the window. He dressed quickly, grabbed his football, and rushed outside. His mother was already up, washing some clothes at the front of the house.

"I'm off now, mum," he shouted. "See you later."

"Have a nice time Kolo," she replied, "and don't get into any trouble!"

"I won't," he said. And he sincerely hoped that he wouldn't.

He passed by Old Man Wilbur, who waved at him.

"Score some goals for me!" he shouted.

Kolo waved and shot off for the large mango tree. He didn't want to be late.

He reached the tree, but no one was there. He knew he was on time, but Midi was nowhere to be seen. He waited for what seemed like thirty minutes but was probably only five.

All his excitement disappeared. Had Midi been playing a trick on him when he told him to meet him here? How could someone be so unkind? he thought.

Kolo could feel his anger rising in him, like a volcano about to explode: 'If I ever see him again, I'll..."

"Hey, Kolo, up here!"

Midi was up in the mango tree - of course, he was! Kolo felt more than a little foolish, but thankfully he hadn't said what he had been thinking out loud.

Midi made his way down the tree and grabbed Kolo around the shoulders.

"Come on," he said, "let's go."

He led Kolo through the bushes and some avocado trees, past the field where the cows were grazing (they were *still* eating!) and down through a small row of even more mango trees. At the end of the row of trees, they turned a corner and entered a large playing field. There were boys on the far side in white t-shirts kicking footballs around and doing various stretches.

"That's the Mighty Mangoes!" Midi said. "Come on; we don't want to be late."

The two boys sprinted across the field. Kolo narrowly avoided treading in a cow pat, dodging it to one side, and soon they reached the group of boys.

"Coach!" Midi shouted to the man who was crouched down pumping up footballs, "this is Kolo; he's just moved here. Can he join the team?"

Coach Kato stood up.

"Good morning, Midi," he said. "Morning, Kolo. We're always looking for new players."

Kolo's heart leapt! A new team! He had only been here for two days, and already he was joining a new team!

"I'm a good striker,' Kolo said with excitement. "In my last team, I was the top scorer and also took all the free-kicks and penalties. And I can score with both feet, and...."

"Okay, okay, calm down," said Coach Kato, "we'll see how good you are *and if* you can fit into our team. You can join us for training today."

Kolo was a bit confused about the comment Coach Kato had made about him fitting into the team (of course he would, he was a great player!), but he let it go from his mind. He was going to train with a new team - the Mighty Mangoes!

"First, you need to meet all the team," said Coach Kato. "Boys, come over here." The boys gathered together

34

one by one, although some quicker than others – two just continued to pass the ball to one another as if they hadn't heard, while another was practising keep-ups, and one was doing a handstand!

Eventually, they all gathered around Coach Kato, and he introduced them to Kolo one by one. Kolo couldn't remember all their names, but they all looked different. One was much shorter than the others, while another was very tall and thin. He'll be good at scoring from corners, Kolo thought - and at picking mangoes! Others were between short and tall, but one boy, in particular, was different to all the others.

His name was Hami, and he only had one arm. To be precise, he was missing half of his left arm just below his elbow. His face looked familiar, but Kolo was more interested in his missing arm. Kolo was shocked that no one else seemed to notice it, or at least didn't care!

Training went well. It was hard work, but Kolo enjoyed it and especially enjoyed doing a few tricks to impress Coach Kato. The boys were all friendly, and most of them were good players; even Hami, who was missing an arm, tried his best, but he could never be a regular player, thought Kolo, not with one arm.

After training had finished, they all sat together and ate the mangoes they had picked from the trees nearby. Kolo assumed the team was called the Mighty Mangoes because of all the mango trees around – the place was full of them!

As they were eating and talking, Coach Kato called Kolo to one side and led him to sit down together on the trunk of an old mango tree that had fallen down the year before.

"So, how did you enjoy your first training session?" Coach Kato asked.

"It was great; I can't wait to play in matches and tournaments. Thanks for allowing me to play."

"And what do you think of the team? Do you like them? Some are a bit cheeky at times, but they're all good boys."

"They all seem nice," Kolo said, "but can I ask a question? Why is Hami in the team? I don't want to sound unkind, but he can't really play football with one arm, can he?"

Coach Kato looked very sad and paused for a moment before speaking.

"Hami is one of the most committed and hard-working members of our team. And yes, he *is* a member of our team. He is always the first to arrive for training, he always helps me to organise the cones and the bibs, and he has a determination that all my players would do well to have. Hami has had to live with his disability, but he has not let it stop him. It's made him even more determined, stronger, and more courageous. He may be restricted in some ways, but his commitment and attitude should be an example to everyone. And yes, he *can* play football, and is actually a very good player..."

He seemed to be getting annoyed and paused for a moment to cool down before beginning again.

"Listen, Kolo, you are clearly a good player, but in my team, I don't just want good players; I want good people.

36

I want people who can see beyond the differences of others and see what they *can* contribute, not what they *can't*. All the players love Hami and are inspired by his commitment and attitude. He is a valuable member of the team. When I met you this morning, I said I'd see if you could fit into our team, and I'm not sure you can. You did lots of nice tricks when we were training, but you seemed more interested in showing off than working for the team, and now you think Hami shouldn't be part of the team because he is missing half of one of his arms! I'm sorry, but those aren't the kind of people I want in my team."

Kolo felt terrible. In fact, he felt all sorts of things. He felt annoyed, he felt upset, he felt embarrassed. And he was sorry.

"I'm sorry, coach. I'll do better next time, I promise," he said.

"I'm going to have to think about having you as part of our team Kolo. I'll let you know my decision when we train again tomorrow evening. Come around then, and we'll talk some more."

Midi and Kolo walked back to the large mango tree, where they would then go their separate ways home.

"How was training then?" asked Midi, "It will be great for us to be playing together."

Kolo just kept quiet. What could he say? Just then, they heard footsteps behind them.

"Wait up, you two." It was Hami, who had been helping Coach Kato pack the equipment and balls away.

"Come on then," said Midi. "He's always the last to leave."

"Oh, by the way, you must have realised by now, Hami's my twin brother."

Commitment

1. What did you think about the story?

2. Was Kolo right to question whether Hami should be part of the team?

3. How do you think Midi might feel if he knew what Kolo had said?

4. What good qualities did you see in Hami?

5. Why do you think Coach Kato reacted the way he did?

6. Do you know anyone who has certain challenges like Hami? How do you treat them?

7. What should Kolo do next?

Kolo and the Mighty Mangoes

Chapter 4

KOLO AND THE WOBBLY BICYCLE

Kolo said goodbye to Midi and Hami. He had hardly said a word as they had walked back from training and couldn't get away fast enough.

All sorts of thoughts and fears raced through Kolo's head, so much so that it was hard to even concentrate on where he was walking, and he walked into a puddle on more than one occasion. What would Midi think of him for being so unkind about his twin brother? And what would Hami himself think? And would Coach Kato tell them?

Midi had been such a good friend to him, and Hami was really nice too. Why did he never stop to think before he did or said anything!? He'd just made friends; he'd just trained with a new football team – and almost as quickly, he was throwing it away.

Maybe he could just do better in future? Maybe Midi and Hami would never know what he had said and thought? Yes, maybe it would be okay just to keep quiet and pretend it never happened. But then what if Coach Kato didn't allow him to join the team? They would ask why, and he'd have to tell them, and then they'd hate him, and then, and then, and then...

Kolo was almost certain his head was about to explode!

By the time he got near to his house, he was exhausted from all the thinking and worrying, not to mention the training session. All he wanted to do was go to sleep and hope it was all a bad dream.

"So how was training, young man?" shouted Old Man Wilbur, "Did you win the cup?" he said and let out a little chuckle.

Kolo really didn't want to talk to him, or anyone else for that matter, but he didn't want to be rude. That would only cause him more problems.

"Oh, it was okay," he said, quickening up his walk, so he didn't have to say anything else.

"You don't sound very happy." Old Man Wilbur said. "You look like someone's pulled your mouth down at the sides. Come and sit with me for a bit; I'm sure it can't be that bad."

It *was* that bad, Kolo thought, but he couldn't refuse to sit with the old man. That would be doubly rude.

He sat down on the concrete step next to Old Man Wilbur, and after a little encouragement, Kolo shared the whole story.

"Don't tell my mum, will you," he said to Old Man Wilbur as he finished the story.

"Oh, I think we can keep this between ourselves for now," he smiled, "but there are some people you do need to talk to. You need to talk to Midi and Hami."

"No!" exclaimed Kolo, so loud he made Old Man Wilbur jump – and Old man Wilbur didn't have good hearing!

"I can't do that. They'll hate me."

"Maybe," said Old Man Wilbur, recovering, "but if you don't, you'll hate yourself more, and you'll always be worried that what you have done will come out in another way. It's always best to say sorry and ask for forgiveness. It might not be as bad as you think."

Kolo knew Old Man Wilbur was right. He had to find Midi and Hami.

He walked back to the large mango tree – after all, that was always where he had met Midi before, but he wasn't there. Kolo even checked up in the tree this time, but he was nowhere to be seen.

He walked back to the playing area, through the bushes and avocado trees, and past where the cows were grazing, but there was no one there except for a small group of boys playing football with an empty plastic bottle.

He walked further, beyond the field and towards the shops and bakery where his mother was to begin work on Monday.

There was a river at one side and a swampy area just in front of it where he could hear the sound of frogs croaking. He went to look down and see if he could see any frogs, or perhaps some fish in the river, but there was nothing. Only a horrible smell coming up from the swamp.

Just as he turned from the swamp, he saw his neighbour, the one with the bicycle and whose wife had big curly hair. He was riding his bicycle towards him, but it was wobbling all over the road, and Kolo quickly saw the reason why. He was carrying a huge sack of something tied to a flat platform over the back wheel, and it was obviously very, very heavy.

As he rode closer towards Kolo, the bicycle wobbled more and more, and Kolo ran across the other side of the road to give his neighbour room.

"Hello, Kolo!!!" the man shouted as he passed by. He removed his hand from the handlebars to wave.

That was a BIG mistake. Without a good grip on the handlebars, the bicycle wobbled more and more, and before Kolo could shout, "Don't fall in the swamp!" the man, his bicycle and the very, very heavy sack of something, all fell into the swamp!

Kolo quickly ran across the road to assess the situation. It was not good. The man was almost upside down, and his bicycle was stuck thick in the swamp with only its back tyre sticking up, looking a bit like the fin of a shark. The very, very heavy bag of something was the only thing that looked in reasonable shape. It had somehow come off the bicycle and landed on a clump of firm ground conveniently positioned in one part of the swamp.

Kolo looked around for something to help rescue the man and found a rope that had been used to tie a cow for grazing but had been left at the side of the road. It looked strong enough and was just about long enough for it to reach the man if they both stretched, but the man seemed to be sinking deeper into the swamp.

"Catch this," Kolo called out and threw the rope towards the man. He leant as far as he could, but the rope was just too short.

Just then, Midi and Hami and the very tall boy from the team (who Kolo thought would be good at both corners and picking mangoes) came walking along. They were carrying things from the shop that they had been sent to buy by their parents.

"Quick, help me!" Kolo called out, and the three boys ran over to see what was happening. "I can't get the rope to reach," said Kolo, "my arms are too short." "Let me try," said the tall boy, whose arms were much longer.

He took the rope and leaned out while Midi held him around the waist to make sure he also didn't fall in. It worked! The man grabbed the rope. Kolo held Midi round the waist, and Hami held Midi by a belt ring on his shorts, and after a count of three, they all pulled, and pulled, and pulled.

Eventually, with lots of pulling and lots of noise, the man began to slowly rise out of the swamp. Once he was part way up, he grabbed his bicycle with one of his hands and began to pull that out with him too – this took a lot more pulling from the boys on the side of the swamp and caused a lot more noise, but eventually, they pulled the man, and his bicycle, out of the swamp!

Both looked incredibly dirty and were incredibly smelly. But they were out.

The only problem now was that the sack of something very, very heavy was sitting on its own little island. Fortunately, the man said he had friends with wooden planks that could help him make a bridge across the swamp, and it would be easy to get the sack back later. What he (and his bicycle) needed right now, he added, was a bath!

He thanked the boys for all their help and walked off, pushing his bicycle and leaving a trail of smelly swamp mud and confused looks from everyone he passed by.

"Well, that was good training," said Midi, "My muscles should be twice the size after that!"

"Thanks for helping," Kolo said.

"No problem," the tall boy said, "but I have to go; my father will be wondering where I am with the tea leaves."

He ran off, leaving Kolo with just Midi and Hami. Now was his opportunity to talk to them.

"While you're here... erm... can I er... talk to you about... something?" he stammered.

"Yes, of course," said Hami, "It sounds important."

The three sat down in the shade of a mango tree (what else?), and Kolo slowly, and with a lot of stops and starts, told them about what he'd thought and said about Hami.

The twins listened but never looked angry. They just looked upset and disappointed. Kolo said how sorry he was, how he still wanted to be friends, and could they forget the whole thing?

Hami was the first to speak.

46

"I can't say I'm not upset, Kolo. I've had to face lots of funny comments and abuse from people just because I'm different, but we're all different in different ways, and it doesn't mean we can't do things together. In the Mighty Mangoes, we all bring different things to the team, and together we achieve a lot – even though we contribute differently. Just now, we were able to help that man because one of us had the good wisdom to find a rope, another could make it reach because of his long arms, and the others were strong enough to be able to pull. Actually, I'm probably the strongest out of all of us because I've built up the strength in my one arm! We need each other and should respect one another – that's real teamwork!"

Kolo realised how right Hami was and promised he'd not be so foolish in future. Midi and Hami agreed that he had indeed been foolish, but they forgave him anyway!

"Oh, and just so you know," said Hami, "I'm not very good at throw-ins, and I'm not great in goal, but there's only a 50% chance of me giving a free-kick away because of handball!"

The three boys looked at each other – and then burst out laughing!

Teamwork

1. What did you like about the story?

2. What can you learn about how the boys helped the man who fell into the swamp?

3. What do you think about the way Hami responded to Kolo's apology?

4. Do you agree with what Hami said about being able to achieve things better together?

5. Have you ever been in a situation when you've had to be honest with someone, even when it's hard to do?

6. What lessons can we learn about how we view, value and treat other people?

7. Do you think Coach Kato should allow Kolo to join the Mighty Mangoes?

Chapter 5

KOLO AND THE BANG BANG BANANAS

After rescuing Kolo's neighbour and his bicycle from the swamp, the boys rested and talked for a while until Midi suddenly remembered the salt he and Hami had been sent to buy and which *their* mother was waiting for!

"We have to go! I forgot about the salt!" he suddenly announced, and both he and Hami leapt up.

"We'll see you tomorrow evening at training," said Midi, and the boys sprinted off as quickly as they could.

'Tomorrow', thought Kolo, 'that's when Coach Kato is going to tell me if I can join the team.'

The excitement of 'the man and his wobbly bicycle' rescue suddenly disappeared and was replaced again with that horrible feeling of worry. In Kolo's mind, tomorrow evening was so far away, but he would just have to wait and be patient.

When he reached home, he saw his neighbour with the wobbly bicycle. He was just finishing washing it down, and both he and the bicycle looked much cleaner than the last time he had seen them. There was still a slight stinky swamp smell in the air, though, although Kolo couldn't tell if that was the bicycle, or the man, or both – or him!

"Kolo," the man shouted across to him, "Thanks again for your help. You're a good boy!"

Kolo waved at his neighbour and then went inside the house.

"Kolo! What is that smell?" his mother said, "go and bathe before you come in here again!"

Kolo had his answer – it was him.

The next day went so slowly, and Kolo had so many thoughts and concerns going around his head about his meeting with Coach Kato. He was outside sweeping around the front of the house when Old Man Wilbur called him over for another talk. Old Man Wilbur could tell he was troubled, and it didn't take long for Kolo to explain things.

"Well, Kolo," Old Man Wilbur said, "there's not much you can do until you meet with Coach Kato, and worrying about it will not change a single thing. You just have to try and be calm. The way we think and feel, our emotions, if you like, can be very odd at times, and we need to keep a close eye on them just to make sure we stay well. I've lived many years on this earth, and I've never seen anything good come from worrying about something you have no control over. What I do know, however, is that you spoke to your friends and that you helped to rescue our neighbour from his rather funny mishap..."

At this point, he let out a huge laugh that almost made him fall off his stool, and he had to grab hold of Kolo's arm to steady himself. Once he'd calmed down, he carried on.

"...I also know that Coach Kato is a good man and will be impressed with how you've behaved regarding those two things."

"But how will he know? And how did *you* know for that matter?" Kolo asked.

"Kolo, you can't do anything in this community without people getting to know. That's why it's always wise to do the right thing, but you're a good boy, and we all make mistakes. The important thing is to take responsibility for them and to learn from them, and I think you've done that."

Kolo felt a bit better after talking to Old Man Wilbur but was still shaking inside when the time came for him to meet with Coach Kato that evening at training.

Coach Kato told Kolo to sit to one side while he gave instructions to the other boys. He told one of the boys, Bululu, to take charge of the warm-up, and Kolo assumed that he must be the team captain. When he'd finished giving his instructions, he sat down next to Kolo.

"Now, Kolo," he said, "you know I was disappointed in you when you came for training last time, and honestly, I didn't think you would fit in the team..." He paused briefly and then continued.

"But I have since learnt about how you talked with Hami and asked him to forgive you, and how you and the others

51

helped to rescue the man and his bicycle from the swamp..."

At this point, he also laughed at the thought of the man upside down in the swamp, but not quite as much as Old Man Wilbur.

"...and you know, now I actually think you can fit perfectly in the team!" Kolo's heart leapt – was he hearing right? Was he really in the team!?

"What I want in the team is boys who can learn from their mistakes, those who can ask for forgiveness when they've done or said something wrong, and those who can show consideration for others. You made quite a bad impression on me at first, Kolo, but since then, you've shown me all those good qualities! And you showed great teamwork and team spirit to rescue that man from the swamp." At which point he laughed again before concluding their brief meeting.

"Go and warm up with the others."

The next few weeks went well. Kolo trained hard with the team and got to know more of the players, including Bululu, who was indeed the captain, Shoopa, who was a striker (and who they nicknamed 'Shoopa the Shooter') and Mufupi, who was a defender, and whose father was a policeman.

He also learnt that the tall boy who had helped them get the man out of the swamp was called 'Giraffe'. He was pretty sure that wasn't his real name and was most likely because he was so tall compared to the rest of them, but 'Giraffe" didn't mind being called 'Giraffe' so that was okay.

Kolo's mother started work at the bakery and would sometimes be allowed to bring fresh bread home for them to eat, and which they'd also share with Old Man Wilbur.

Kolo started school and enjoyed it, although his mother didn't always have money for the fees, and so he had to miss it sometimes - or sneak in and hide at the back!

Some things stayed the same; Old Man Wilbur still sat on his stool outside his house waving at people passing by and laughing, and Kolo's sister still enjoyed sitting in the washing basin, so much so in fact, that his mother had had to buy a new one – just to do the washing in!

One day at training, Coach Kato had an announcement - The Mighty Mangoes were going to play in this year's regional tournament! All the boys were incredibly excited and started cheering, clapping and jumping around!

Last year the team hadn't been able to enter as they didn't have the money for the registration fees, but this year Coach Kato shared with the boys that Mr Dough, who owned the bakery, had agreed to sponsor them. This news, of course, resulted in more dancing and the boys shouting: "Mr Dough, Mr Dough, Mr Dough..." at the top of their voices.

To say the boys were excited was an understatement and Kolo felt the most excited of them all. He was going to play in his first tournament with The Mighty Mangoes.

The tournament consisted of two mini-leagues, with the top two teams from the league stages going into the semi-finals and then the winners from there going into the final.

Training for the matches started straight away, and within another two weeks, their first match was announced.

"Right boys," said Coach Kato, "I've got the fixtures for the league matches, and our first match, next week, will be against... The Bang Bang Bananas Football Club!"

"Oh noooooooo!" the entire team groaned. The *entire* team.

"What's wrong?" Kolo whispered to Midi. "Who are the Bang Bang Bananas?"

"Only our biggest rivals and the roughest team around! They're also the biggest cheaters and do all sorts of tricks and funny things to win matches. All they care about is winning – and they certainly don't care about how they do it. The last time we played them they, kicked Bululu so hard he had a lump on his leg for weeks the size of an egg."

It would be a tough opening game, Kolo thought, and indeed it was.

When the day came, Kolo and the rest of the team were really nervous. They knew the Bang Bang Bananas always played unfairly, and they suspected that their coach often gave the referee a few coins too - just to make sure they won.

The game was being played at The Mighty Mangoes home ground, Mango Park, and when the Bang Bang Bananas arrived, Kolo almost fell over at the sight of them. They were so tall, and many of them had muscles as big as some of the mangoes around Mango Park.

"Surely they're too big and too old to play against us?" Kolo said to Bululu.

"Yes, they are, but they always get to play for some reason. It will be a tough game, Kolo, but remember to keep your cool and to let your feet do the talking."

It was indeed a tough game. The toughest Kolo had ever known. The Bang Bang Bananas were doing everything they could to win the game; they kicked the Mighty Mango players, pushed them over when the referee wasn't looking, and one of them even pulled down Giraffe's shorts when he jumped up for a header!

They also had supporters on the touchline, mostly their little brothers, who were shouting rude things, and two small boys in particular kept annoying Coach Kato.

The worst thing the Bang Bang Bananas did, however, was to say horrible things. Words can often hurt much more than even the hardest of tackles, and one boy in particular was especially horrible. He was called Smudge and was constantly making fun of Hami for only having one arm - as well as kicking him and pulling his ears when the referee wasn't looking.

It was amazing how Hami just ignored the abuse and stuck to his game, but his brother, Midi, was getting angrier and angrier. Then, when Smudge again kicked Hami when the referee wasn't looking, Midi seemed to lose all control. He ran across the pitch and thumped Smudge straight on the nose – just as the referee turned around!

Smudge's nose exploded, and it looked like a bright red tomato had been squashed in his face. Of course, that wasn't the only red thing. The referee stormed over and had no option but to give Midi a red card! Midi was sent off, and the Mighty Mangoes were down to ten men.

Midi was still furious as he walked off the pitch, and with his head down, he spotted a rotten mango on the ground. He picked it up, and with all his force, threw it at Smudge, where it hit him on the chest and splattered rotten mango juice all over him.

"How's that for a Mighty Mango!!!" Midi yelled and stormed off the pitch.

Patient & Self Controlled

1. Do you think Midi was right to do what he did? What are the reasons why you think this?

2. What might be the consequences of Midi's actions? How might that impact the team?

3. What do you think about how Hami handled the situation?

4. Why did you think Coach Kato allowed Kolo to join the team?

5. Do you agree with what Old Man Wilbur said to Kolo about emotions? What are the reasons why you think this?

6. Have you ever been in any of the situations in the story?

    a. How did you feel?

    b. What did you do?

    c. What were the outcomes?

7. How do you think the match will finish?

Kolo and the Mighty Mangoes

Chapter 6

KOLO, MIDI AND A MANGO CRUSH

The Mighty Mangoes players were stunned. No one had ever seen Midi get so angry, let alone punch someone on the nose!

Even Hami, who had, of course, known him all his life, had never seen him get *that* angry – but he could understand why. The twins had always been loyal and would do anything for each other; Hami imagined it was harder for Midi to see his brother get abused. At least for him, he knew how it felt inside and could deal with it – Midi could only imagine how it felt.

Anyway, whatever had happened, most of the Mighty Mango players were secretly pleased Smudge had got a thump on the nose. He deserved it after all, but now they were a man down and had to work extra hard to get anything from the game.

The Mighty Mangoes put in every effort they had. They were nothing if not determined and committed to the cause, but the Bang Bang Bananas were a tough team. Midi had been sent off midway through the first half, and just before half-time, the Bang Bang Bananas scored a goal, and then about 10 minutes into the second half, they got another – although it was a very lucky one. Mufupi tried to clear the ball for the Mighty Mangoes, only for it to hit the Bang Bang Bananas striker on the back off the head and loop up and into the goal.

"Don't give up, boys. The Mighty Mangoes never give up!" shouted Coach Kato. And it was true. They would fight to the end.

As they were now 2-0 up, the Bang Bang Bananas relaxed a little bit and continued to tease the Mighty Mangoes, trying little flicks and tricks and telling them they were rubbish. Of course, they didn't stop kicking them either, but they seemed to slow down a bit and take things a little bit easy. After all, they had the game won.

The Mighty Mangoes were not finished, though. With time ticking away, they knew it would be hard to win now, but if they could just get a goal...

Then the Mighty Mangoes got a piece of good fortune. The Bang Bang Banana's centre half cut out a through ball aimed at Shoopa, but instead of clearing the ball, he tried to be a bit too clever for his own good. With Shoopa bearing down on him, he turned back inside and attempted to pass the ball back to his goalkeeper. However, he had not seen Kolo, who had taken a chance and snuck in behind him. The pass to the goalkeeper went straight into Kolo's path, and he was clean through with only the goalie to beat.

Kolo took the ball in his stride. His heart was thumping, and he could hear the Bang Bang Bananas players running behind him – they sounded like a herd of elephants, about to squash him, but he knew he just had to focus and keep going.

Forward he went until he was one-on-one with the goalie who was rushing out to meet him.

Now was his chance. He hit the ball as hard as he could towards the corner of the goal; past the goalkeeper it went, and 'smash' into the back of the net!!! He cleverly dodged the 'keeper who was still running towards him and swerved off to the side. The Bang Bang Bananas players who had been chasing him couldn't stop in time and crashed into the goalkeeper, leaving them all in a heap on the floor!

Kolo turned around to find all the Mighty Mango players running towards him, with smiles as wide as watermelon slices! They celebrated together. It was a great goal against all the odds and one that, under the circumstances, was enough for the Mighty Mangoes. Of course, they didn't want to lose, but there were other games to come, and they could still easily qualify for the semi-finals. They were just pleased to get a goal after everything that had happened, and there were only 5 minutes left. To lose 2-1 was no shame in such a game as this.

But football is a funny game.

The Mighty Mangoes continued to play as they had been coached by Coach Kato, with passion, with support for each other, and passing the ball around. They knew no other way.

They were all expecting the final whistle at any moment but gave it one last effort. Mufupi put a long ball over the top for Kolo to run on to, but it was too far for him to reach.

Smudge, who had decided he didn't want to play near Hami anymore because it kept reminding him of his squashed nose and had gone to help the defenders, kicked the ball as hard as he could and out for a corner.

"That must be time now," he growled at the referee. "Blow your whistle!!!"

"The 90 minutes are up," the referee said, "but we have an extra 2 minutes for injuries – mostly from fouls *you* committed! One minute has gone, and as soon as the ball comes back, we'll have one more minute left."

Smudge sniffed and walked off. The game was already won anyway, he thought, what do I care?

Bululu placed the ball down for the corner, and all the Mighty Mango players were in the penalty area or on the edge of the box, hoping for any chance to strike at goal.

Bululu ran up and connected with the ball perfectly, firing it up and towards the box. It went over Kolo, who leapt as high as he could but not quite high enough, then it went over Mufupi just brushing the top of his hair, and also over Hami, who was nowhere near it (although he was one of the smallest players on the team, so he was never going to get to it.)

But then... right at the back ... just when it looked like the ball was going to miss everyone, up jumped 'Giraffe.' He flung his head towards the ball and connected with it brilliantly. There was a loud thud as he headed the ball and then a swish as it hit the back of the net!!!

GOAL!

The Mighty Mangoes went wild. It had been one of their toughest games ever, and they had managed to equalise with just seconds remaining. The Bang Bang Bananas, who looked like they might burst into tears at any moment, only kicked the ball again to restart the game before the referee blew for full time.

The Mighty Mangoes had done it. Final score 2-2.

It was a great result for the Mighty Mangoes. They had shown incredible determination and commitment to not only put up with the Bang Bang Bananas and their dirty tactics but to keep going and finally get the draw.

The only downside, of course, was the incident involving Midi. After he'd been sent off, he had just disappeared. Coach Kato had tried to talk to him, but he was still very angry, so he'd left him alone to cool off. The next time Coach Kato had turned around, Midi had gone.

When he returned home, Kolo explained the whole game to Old Man Wilbur, including how Midi got sent off.

"It was so unlike Midi," he said, "I've never seen him so angry. It was like he just got angrier until he eventually exploded!"

"Hmmm... it does sound *just* like that," said Old Man Wilbur and pointed to the cooking pot outside the house of the man with the wobbly bicycle, where his wife with the big curly hair was preparing food.

"You see that cooking pot over there. We can be a lot like that."

Kolo looked at Old Man Wilbur. For someone usually quite wise, it was a very silly thing to say.

"When you're cooking," he continued, "you have to keep checking on the food, and most especially on the heat. What happens if you leave it boiling for too long and don't pay attention to it?"

Kolo thought for a second, "Well, the food can get spoilt... and the water can boil up and come over the top."

"Exactly!" said Old Man Wilbur and stuck his finger in the air.

"We can all be like that cooking pot. Sometimes our emotions and especially our anger can boil up in us, and we can get hotter and hotter, and without making some adjustments, we too can boil over! I think that's what happened to your friend Midi. I suspect he might have 'cooled' down by now, though, and could probably do with a friend."

"Thanks, Wilbur!!!" Kolo said, and he went off in search of Midi. He had a good idea where he'd be.

As he had suspected, Kolo found Midi sitting in the large mango tree. He refused to come down, however, so Kolo, who wasn't anywhere near as good at climbing trees, had to go up. It was not easy, and he was quite scared at times, but he eventually made it and joined Midi on a thick branch. It had smaller branches growing off it, so Kolo had something to hold on to.

They talked about what had happened; about a boiling cooking pot, about getting angry, and about controlling their emotions. They both agreed it was very hard, especially with the Bang Bang Bananas, but that if you can't keep cool, it can often have bad consequences.

"You nearly lost the match because of me," said Midi, explaining that when he'd got sent off, he'd snuck off and found a mango tree a little further back from the pitch and had watched the rest of the game from there.

"But we didn't! We got an amazing draw!" said Kolo. "I'm not sure any of the Mighty Mangoes would blame you given the circumstances, and we all worked really hard to get back into the game. Yes, what you did was wrong, but I'm sure all the players understand."

Midi felt a bit better and was happy to have a friend like Kolo, but Kolo was not quite correct; not all the players were so forgiving.

At training the next evening, a heated conversation was going on when Midi arrived.

"We had to work extra hard because Midi got sent off, and we would even have won if we had him on the pitch," said one voice.

"But you can't blame him! We all should have punched those stupid bananas!" said another.

"But now he'll be suspended for the next game, and we'll have to work harder again to get through to the semi-final. He's let us down," said the next voice.

"But he's our friend and has done more than enough to help us win games in the past," contributed another.

65

And so the voices went on and on, but no one noticed that Midi had arrived and was hearing everything that was being said, nor that Coach Kato had also arrived and was standing next to Midi with his arm around his shoulder, and which made him feel good.

The debate slowly came to an end as, one by one, the players noticed Midi and Coach Kato standing there.

Midi moved forward to stand in front of his teammates and asked them to sit down. They all sat in a semi-circle as they did at half-time when Coach Kato was giving a team talk and waited for Midi to speak. They were silent, and some of them were feeling slightly ashamed about some of the things they had been saying.

"Look, you're right. All of you are right. I've let you down, and I'm not going to hide that. I could make excuses about being provoked, but I should have been able to control myself, and I'm sorry. I made a mistake, and I have to take responsibility for that. Though I won't play in the next game, I'll do all that I can to support the team, and I'll work extra hard in training, so I'm even better when I come back. I'm sorry. Please forgive me."

Everyone was silent for a few moments.

Bululu was the first to break the silence, though, when he started clapping! Then Mufupi joined in, and of course, Kolo and Hami were not far behind. Soon all the players were clapping Midi. He was their player, their friend, and as one, they were together again.

"Midi, Midi, Midi..." they began shouting, and all leapt up.

"Mango Crush!!!" shouted Bululu, and all the boys surrounded Midi and squeezed together, with him in the middle. He felt SO good. What a team he was part of, he thought, 'even when you mess up, they can forgive you if you're honest and take responsibility.'

Go Mighty Mangoes!

Honest

1. What did you like about the story?

2. Have you ever played in a match like the one the Mighty Mangoes played in with the Bang Bang Bananas? How did you feel during the match? How did you behave?

3. Do you ever get angry as Midi did? Can you reflect on some situations from your own life?

4. What were the consequences of you getting angry?

5. How do you think you can control your anger?

6. It must have been hard for Midi to say sorry and to take responsibility for his actions. Why do you think that was, and would you be able to do the same?

7. What can you learn from the story that you can use in your own life?

8. What do you think will happen next?

Chapter 7

KOLO'S NEW BOOTS

After his sending off for punching Smudge in the face, Midi was given some work to do by Coach Kato as punishment.

Even though the team had forgiven him, he knew that there were always consequences for what people do and say, and he accepted his punishment. He was suspended from training for two sessions, which was indeed a real punishment as all the boys loved to train and play the training matches. He was also made responsible for cleaning out the storeroom. This included making sure all the training equipment was brought out and put back before and after training, and that all the bibs were washed each week. This was the worst part as they were always dirty and sweaty!

Coach Kato trusted Midi with a key to the storeroom, which was a small brick room built near to the playing field, just a few mango trees back. The room used to be a storeroom for a small grinding mill that was there years ago. When the mill closed, it was demolished, but the storeroom was left as the local leaders agreed that the Mighty Mangoes could use it to keep their football equipment in.

Hami was also often given a key for the storeroom, as he was usually the first one there and would get all the equipment organised.

Midi went about his punishment without complaint. He had learnt to keep his emotions in check!

The Mighty Mangoes won their next two games in their mini-league: 2-1 against the Giant Guavas and 3-0 against the Awesome Apples (who were not quite as awesome as their name suggested). Kolo scored another 2 goals, and Midi returned to the team after his suspension, but only as a substitute.

The wins meant that they finished top of their league, with the Bang Bang Bananas finishing second. Both teams would now play in the semi-finals and could only play each other again if they met in the final.

It was all going well for the Mighty Mangoes, until one day they arrived at the training ground to find Coach Kato looking very cross and also very sad.

"I need to talk to you all, boys," he said. "Where are Midi, Hami and Kolo?"

Midi, Hami and Kolo had not arrived, which was unusual for them as they were all normally on time, and Midi, of course, had to be there early to clean the storeroom and organise the equipment and bibs.

No one knew where they were, and Coach Kato said he couldn't wait if they were not coming: he had to tell those who were there the news.

"Someone has entered the storeroom and stolen some footballs and some of my whistles, but as well as that, they have also stolen the cash box where I kept the money for the tournament fees. Without this money, I'm sorry, but we won't be able to continue in the tournament."

The players were shocked. For a moment, they were just silent, and then they erupted with questions that anyone passing by would barely understand as they were all talking at once.

Who would steal money from The Mighty Mangoes, and how did they even know the money was there? And what were they going to do about the tournament? They couldn't ask Mr Dough for more money, and none of them, including Coach Kato, could pay themselves.

Coach Kato eventually brought the noise to a halt.

"The strange thing is," he said, "is that the storeroom wasn't broken into as you'd expect. The padlock was still on the door, and it was even locked as normal. I only realised when I went inside and the place was a mess. Everything was scattered about the room, and those things were gone."

"It must be someone who has a key," Shoopa said.

"Or they could have got through the roof," another said. "Those iron sheets are not that secure. They always make a noise when it's windy - like someone clapping."

They began talking again, but this time not all at once, as the boys threw questions and theories back and forth, and Coach Kato chipped in here and there.

71

"But who has a key, Coach Kato?" Mufupi asked. They all suddenly stopped. Surely not.

Midi had been given a key to clear the storeroom and organise the equipment, and Hami was always in the storeroom as well, and also often had a key. And where were they today? And where was Kolo?

Coach Kato couldn't believe those boys would be responsible for this.

"It couldn't be *anyone* here," he said, "I trust you all, and I trust those boys."

"But where are they?" asked Bululu. "Why are they not here?"

It was a good question and one that no one could answer.

"Look, let's train anyway," said Coach Kato. "Time is going, and we still have enough balls and equipment to use. We'll work out what to do later, and training will take our minds off things. Let's just keep this to ourselves for now. If the thieves are around, we don't want them to hear us talking about it."

The boys agreed, got up and turned to move into the field. Just as they did, though, they saw a figure running across from the other side of the field. It was Kolo.

"I'm sorry I'm late, coach," he said, panting for breath like a dog who had just been chasing a really fast cat.

"That's okay...we're... just about... to start training," said Coach Kato slowly. His eyes, and indeed each pair of eyes of all the Mighty Mangoes, were staring at Kolo's feet.

"Oh, these are my new boots," he said. "They're smart, aren't they?"

They were *indeed* smart. They looked brand new and were a shiny blue, with a thin white stripe down the side. They looked expensive, like the boots they'd seen professional players wearing on the few occasions the boys had watched a match on television.

Coach Kato, and all the boys, in fact, knew that Kolo's mother could not afford to buy them for him, and no one else in the team had boots like them. Some of the players didn't even have boots at all, and substitutes often had to use the boots of a player coming off during matches.

It was only a matter of time before someone asked the question they were all thinking.

"So, where did you get them from?" Mosi asked. "They must have been expensive? Where did you get the money for them?"

Kolo looked uncomfortable.

"Er... someone gave them to me," he said.

"Who?" asked Bululu.

"Erm... I can't tell you. I'm sorry." Kolo looked even more uncomfortable. "But we can all share them. At least, anyone whose feet are the same size as mine."

"No thanks," said Bululu and turned away. The rest of the team followed their captain to the centre of the field to warm up.

Kolo felt bad. He could see they were not happy, but he

joined them in the centre of the field and trained as normal. Although actually, it wasn't normal at all.

The other boys didn't speak to him and certainly didn't joke with him like usual. Some of the tackles were also a bit rougher, and Coach Kato had to calm the boys down at times.

Kolo knew it was because of the football boots but didn't know what to do.

After training, he said goodbye to the rest of the team, although no one really replied, and made his way home.

"It *must* be him," said Bululu to the others after Kolo had left. "There's no way he could afford those boots, and he was really funny when I asked him where he'd got them from."

"Yeah," agreed Shoopa, "and where are Midi and Hami today? They're the only ones who have keys to the storeroom, and now they haven't come for training? It's very suspicious!"

Bululu spoke again: "Yes, Midi and Hami must have seen the cash box when they were in the store. They must have found it while cleaning and moving things around; I know Coach Kato keeps it well hidden."

"Then they'd agreed with Kolo to steal the money. Those three are always together," added Mufupi, who felt he was probably the best one of them all for solving crimes because his father was a policeman.

"But how could they do that to us?" said Bululu. "We've always been there for one another, and now we can't even

74

compete in the tournament because of those thieves! It must be Kolo. He's only been here five minutes, and he's caused problems. Midi and Hami were good before he came. I used to like him, and he's a good player, but now I see the real him – he's a snake and a thief!"

When Kolo reached home, Old Man Wilbur, as always, was sitting outside his house on his little wooden stool. It was almost automatic now that Kolo would walk over and sit with him.

He shared about how odd it had been at training and how the boys had behaved strangely towards him because of his new football boots.

"They were probably jealous," said Old Man Wilbur, "boys can be like that, and girls for that matter... and grown-ups too when you think about it. Where *did* you get the boots from, by the way?"

Again, Kolo felt uncomfortable.

"I can't tell you," he said, "I'm sorry."

"Ah, and there might be your problem, Kolo. It's not always good to have secrets."

The next day was one of the worst days Kolo had ever known. He knew people were talking about him. People he was normally friends with turned their backs on him and stopped talking when he came close to them – and then would begin talking again when he went past.

He could hear people whispering things about him and giving him tough looks with their faces, their eyes slightly closed, and their mouths pinched together as if they were trying desperately not to let bad words come out.

Worst of all were his teammates from The Mighty Mangoes, who ignored him completely.

Even walking home from school, people would look at him and shake their heads. Women talking at the borehole would nod their heads towards him as if to say, 'That's him.'

It was horrible! What had he done? And all because of a pair of football boots.

His mother had left for the bakery early in the morning before Kolo had got up and gone to school, but he knew she would certainly have heard the talk going around, and he would be in *real* trouble when she returned home in the evening.

"Kolo, I need to talk to you," said Old Man Wilbur as Kolo reached home.

Kolo walked across. If he only had one friend left in the world, it was probably going to be Old Man Wilbur.

"I've heard you've done a terrible, terrible thing, Kolo," Old Man Wilbur said.

For the first time that Kolo had ever known it, Old Man Wilbur was not smiling.

"Tell me what you have done and why. And remember, it is always best to be honest."

Team Talk - Communication

1. Did you like the story?

2. What did you like or dislike about it?

3. Have you ever been tempted to steal something? Have you ever been in the position of:

   a. Kolo.

   b. The other Mighty Mangoes players.

4. What was it like, and how did you feel?

5. Were the Mighty Mangoes players right to treat Kolo the way they did?

6. How do you think the whole community got to hear about things?

7. Why do you think Midi and Hami didn't go to training that day?

8. What do you think Kolo should do next?

9. How can Kolo restore his relationship with his Mighty Mangoes teammates?

10. What do you think will happen next?

Kolo and the Mighty Mangoes

Chapter 8

KOLO'S SIDE OF THE STORY

Kolo took a deep breath and began to share what had happened.

"I didn't realise it would cause so many problems. And now everyone is ignoring me and whispering about me because of it. I can't imagine what it would be like if I did something really bad," he said. He was almost in tears.

"But Kolo, it's not about you wearing your new boots," said Old Man Wilbur. "The Mighty Mangoes storeroom was broken into, and *money* was stolen! Everyone thinks it's you because of your new boots and because you won't tell anyone where you got them from!"

"WHAT?" cried Kolo. "I haven't stolen anything! It isn't true!"

"Then where did you get the money for the boots, and why were you late for training? And where are Midi and Hami?"

Kolo took another deep breath, and this time, told Old Man Wilbur *everything*.

The man with the wobbly bicycle who he had helped to rescue from the swamp had given Kolo the boots as a 'thank you' gift for helping him. They used to belong to his nephew, who lived with the man's brother in the city. His feet had grown too big for them, and so when the man with the wobbly bicycle had visited, he asked if he could have them. 'I know just the person for these,' he'd said.

He had cleaned the boots up and made them look as good as new and had then given them to Kolo.

"I know you like football, and I'm very grateful to you for helping me, so I want you to have these," he had said, but then added: "...but please don't tell anyone where you got them from. Of course, there were four of you who helped me, and I don't have boots for you all. And also, I don't want half the children in the village knocking on my door asking for football boots!"

Kolo had agreed to keep quiet, which was why he'd been so uncomfortable when people had asked where they had come from. He didn't want to betray the man's trust, and he thought he was doing the right thing. He had no idea about the break-in at the storeroom. Of course, no one was talking to him, so there was no way he would know. He was late for the training session that day because he'd been waiting for Midi at the large mango tree where they always met.

He told Old Man Wilbur everything; how he had arrived late for training and how the boys had been jealous of him and rude to him. He told him how much he regretted wearing the boots and had realised that it was insensitive because lots of the other boys don't have boots, and those

80

that do, have boots that are split or torn. And that no one had boots like his.

He'd been waiting and waiting, but Midi had not shown up, so he decided he'd just go to training on his own. Maybe Midi was already there?

On his way home, he'd gone to Midi's house to see if he was okay, but also to tell him about how people had been odd with him at training.

Midi's mother told Kolo that both he and Hami were sick.

"They always do things together, those two," she'd joked. "They'll be fine, though; they just need to rest for a few days."

Kolo said he'd thought little about what had happened at training since then, only that he'd talk to his teammates and apologise if it looked like he was showing off.

Then people had been unkind to him at school and everywhere in the community in fact!

"I didn't steal the money, honestly," he said. "It's a big mistake!"

"Oh goodness," said Old Man Wilbur when Kolo had finished. "It does indeed sound like a big mistake, and a terrible one at that!"

"I told you before, Kolo, that you can't keep things quiet in this community. It seems like your teammates have completely got the wrong end of the stick, and rumours have spread like wildfire! Sadly, many people here like a good rumour and enjoy gossiping about the bad of someone else!

I suppose it makes them feel better about themselves and all the wrong things *they* do, but it's certainly not right."

"So, what do we do?" said Kolo. "Everyone hates me and thinks I'm a thief!"

"Well, first of all, you need to calm down. As I told you, news moves fast around here, and I'm sure we can ensure the *real* story spreads just as quickly."

Old Man Wilbur told Kolo to go and get the man with the wobbly bicycle.

"He's the one who's caused this pickle," he said, "though totally unintentionally, of course."

Kolo went across to the house of the man with the wobbly bicycle. No one answered the door when he knocked, so he went around to the back where the man's wife (with the big curly hair) was hanging out some washing. Kolo shared the story with her.

"Oh my!!!" she exclaimed. "What a pickle! (Pickle seemed to be the word of the day.) Unfortunately, my husband has gone away for a few days visiting his brother. He called the other day, and then he just rushed off. It seemed quite urgent. He didn't go on his bicycle, though – it's way too far for that!"

She laughed at her little joke but then stopped abruptly, realising that Kolo wasn't laughing, and it probably wasn't a laughing matter anyway.

"He'll be back in the morning, though. I'm sure we'll sort out this little pickle, my dear," she said. Yes, 'pickle' surely *was* the word of the day.

82

Kolo explained things to Old Man Wilbur, who suggested they just sit and wait. The night would soon come and then the morning after that.

Old Man Wilbur also told Kolo he would 'arrest' his mother on her way home from the bakery and tell her everything before she got a chance to shout at Kolo! 'Arrest' didn't seem the most appropriate word given the circumstances, but he was grateful for Old Man Wilbur's help.

Old Man Wilbur did indeed stop Kolo's mother on her way home. She was all flustered and half-running, half-walking, as she made her way around the corner. She had heard the rumours and was in such a terrible state at the bakery that she'd almost sat down on a freshly baked loaf. She couldn't wait to get home and find out exactly what Kolo had done now!

Old Man Wilbur shared everything, and Kolo's mother slowly returned to normal. As far as Kolo knew, she didn't mention 'pickle', but she did tell him she was relieved it had all been a mistake and gave Kolo one of her biggest ever hugs when she finally reached home.

"It will be okay, Kolo. Don't worry," she said. And it was.

The next morning the man with the wobbly bicycle returned from his trip, carrying another very, very heavy sack of something, but not this time on his wobbly bicycle. As soon as his wife (with the big curly hair) had updated him, he rushed across to Kolo, who had been waiting outside ever since the sun had come up that morning.

"Oh, I'm so sorry, Kolo!" he said. "I was trying to do the right thing, and then I did the wrong thing instead. I'm always doing that! Or at least that's what my wife keeps telling me! We'll fix this, though, don't you worry."

He then rushed off to his house and came back with a handheld megaphone, like the type policemen use when they need to tell a lot of people off all at once.

He got on his bicycle and wobbled off. Kolo smiled, looking at the man wobbling again, but as he was riding with one hand on the handlebars and the other holding the megaphone, he thought that was a good enough excuse to be wobbling this time.

The man rode off, and Kolo could hear him shouting into the megaphone.

"Special meeting today at 5 pm at Mango Park! Everyone must attend and especially The Mighty Mangoes Football Team!"

Kolo could hear the message being amplified through the megaphone long after the man disappeared. He didn't know what was going to happen at the meeting later that day, but he felt very happy that he'd been able to talk to Old Man Wilbur and then the man with the wobbly bicycle and that the truth about the whole horrible thing was hopefully going to come out.

His mother told him to stay at home from school that day. She didn't want any more trouble for him, and so instead, he spent the day talking to Old Man Wilbur.

Until 5 pm that is, when it was time for the meeting...

Relationship

1. What did you think of the story?

2. What do you think about how people treated Kolo?

3. How did you feel when the truth came out that Kolo had done nothing wrong?

4. What should Kolo do now?

5. Who do you think broke into the storehouse and stole the money?

6. Have you ever been accused of something you haven't done or accused someone of something they haven't done? How did it feel?

7. What lessons can we learn from the story?

8. What do you think will happen at the special meeting at Mango Park?

Kolo and the Mighty Mangoes

Chapter 9

KOLO'S DISCOVERY

Kolo was incredibly nervous. He stood next to the man with the wobbly bicycle on a raised piece of land where people always spoke from during community meetings and looked out at the people who had gathered at Mango Park.

There were lots of them, including all the Mighty Mango players and Coach Kato.

Midi and Hami were not there as far as Kolo could see; they were probably still resting, but their mother was there, wearing her best dress and with a bright red scarf tied around her head.

The man with the wobbly bicycle placed his arm around Kolo's shoulder and held the megaphone to his mouth. Kolo was surprised he didn't wobble, but he didn't. 'Maybe it's just on bicycles?' he thought.

"Attention! Attention!" he shouted into the megaphone, and the crowd slowly quietened down.

Once he had their attention, he put the megaphone down. The crowd was a good size, but it was hardly the

World Cup Final, and he knew he could continue just using his voice.

"This young man here," he told the crowd, "Is NOT the one responsible for the break-in at the Mighty Mangoes storeroom and is certainly NOT a thief!"

The crowd murmured to one another, and the noise level began to rise again, so much so that the man with the wobbly bicycle needed his megaphone to get their attention again, but once he did, he explained the whole story.

He also shared how he'd gone to see Coach Kato, who had confirmed to him the time when the break-in must have happened, and how Kolo had been at home that very evening washing clothes.

Midi and Hami's mother also announced that it couldn't have been her boys either, as they were both unwell and at home at that time.

Coach Kato then spoke up and confirmed it couldn't have been anyone from the Mighty Mangoes team.

"There's more chance of an *actual* mango breaking in than those boys," he said, and everybody laughed.

"I think we all owe Kolo an apology," said the man with the wobbly bicycle, "and I'm also sorry for being a part of this whole confusion. I'm a bit of a foolish thing at times and don't always think things through!"

Everyone laughed again, and then, in another period of noise, they shouted their apologies to Kolo. Kolo couldn't hear them all but could certainly feel that he was loved again. Some people put their hands to their chests and bowed their heads slightly as a sign of apology. Others waved to him, and of course, many of them just shouted – including the Mighty Mango players who felt the worst out of all the people there.

"Oh, and another thing," the man with the bicycle shouted, bringing the noise to an end again. "I almost forgot. I was away these last few days, which is why I couldn't sort this whole mess out before. I was away visiting my brother again – the one who gave me the boots for Kolo. He called me and said I must go there immediately. After he had given me the football boots for Kolo, he mentioned it to his friends, and they also said they had boots that were too small for their boys now – and they mentioned it to *their* friends, and they... Anyway, look at this!"

He lifted the big sack that Kolo had seen him return with that morning and emptied its contents.

Football boot after football boot rolled out of the bag, like a waterfall!

"We've got boots for all the Mighty Mangoes!!!!"

The crowd cheered! The Mighty Mangoes players high-fived each other and then jumped around as if safari ants were biting their feet, and Kolo felt on top of the world!

"Thank you," he said and flung his arms around the man with the bicycle. Often boys would laugh at something like that, but no one seemed to care.

"You're welcome, Kolo," said the man with the wobbly bicycle. "It's the least I could do."

The celebrations eventually died down, and the crowd started to disperse. Everyone was happy that things had worked out well, and they'd all learned a valuable lesson about gossiping. A question remained, however, that they had all seemed to have forgotten. It was Mrs Threading, a rather large lady who had a tailoring business, who raised it with the crowd.

"But if it wasn't Kolo or any of the other Mighty Mangoes, then who *did break* in?"

It was a very good question, and the Mighty Mangoes were determined to find out.

After the meeting, the Mighty Mangoes players apologised personally to Kolo. They were very sorry and felt so bad for the things they'd said and thought.

"Well, it did look suspicious, I suppose," said Kolo, "but I could never do that, and you shouldn't just jump to conclusions without finding out the real facts." The boys agreed.

"We've learnt our lesson, Kolo," Bululu said. "We'll never do the same again."

Kolo smiled. He was just happy that things had been dealt with and the team were as one again.

"What can we do to make things better?" said Mufupi.

"There's nothing really," said Kolo, "I'm just happy we're friends again. Let's just put it behind us and find out who really stole the money!"

"You're right. Thanks, Kolo," said Bululu. "But there's one thing we *must* do first," he added, "MANGO CRUSH!!!!!"

The boys rushed around Kolo and hugged him. They squeezed him so much he wondered if he might actually end up as mighty mango juice, but it felt so good to be loved and valued again. Eventually, the boys collapsed in a heap on the floor and laughed until their cheeks hurt.

Things were good again, and there was more good news for Kolo and the Mighty Mangoes over the next couple of days. Mr Dough had heard what had happened and offered to add a little more money to replace some of what had been stolen. He was disappointed that the money had not been taken better care of but was very impressed with how it had all been sorted out – even if the money was still missing. Mr Dough couldn't give a lot of extra money, but it would at least allow them to pay the fees for their semi-final match against the Power Pack Pineapples.

The boys and Coach Kato were delighted and offered to give Mr Dough some help at the bakery if he needed it.

"What a wonderful team you are," said Mr Dough when Bululu (as team captain) had gone to see him and to offer their help, "and such team spirit and consideration for others! I do indeed have some work you can help me with. Thank you!"

Mr Dough had a storeroom at the back of the bakery that was full of old junk – broken bicycle wheels, cracked cooking pots, an old clock which was missing most of the numbers, and lots of other dirty, cracked and broken things.

"It would be great if you could help me clean this room out, boys; it's a bit of a mess, I'm afraid. I've kept all these broken things over the years, hoping they'd be useful for something, but they're just taking up space. I want to use this room for storing my bakery tools and machines, so it needs a good clean out."

"No problem, Mr Dough," said Kolo, "we'll have this done in no time."

It would actually take longer than Kolo or any of them expected. It was a big room, but they worked hard together as a team, offering their different skills to get the work done.

'Giraffe' was able to reach up high to grab things that were piled on top of each other, and he could use his long arms to get into difficult spaces, and Mufupi and Mosi, as two of the smallest players, were able to get into places others couldn't squeeze in and helped push things forward for them to grab hold of. Meanwhile, Shoopa and Nakati kept everyone entertained, making jokes and putting things like saucepans and basins on their heads!

Hami also played a big part; he might only have had one arm, but it was the strongest arm in the team.

The Mighty Mangoes worked mightily together, and bit by bit, they started to make an impact on the storeroom.

As they collected the dirty, cracked and broken items, they took them outside and placed them in an area a little distance away, from where Mr Dough said a truck would eventually come to take them. The area was a bit far from the storeroom, but Bululu had told them it would be good training carrying the things, and they'd all agreed.

During the clean-up, Kolo and Shoopa were carrying an old table together to the collection point (it only had three legs and was bent in the middle like a very old man) when they heard some voices not far away behind the corner of a row of shops. They couldn't see anyone because the voices were coming from behind the shops, but Kolo recognised one of the voices. It was Smudge from the Bang Bang Bananas.

"Shhh," Kolo said to Shoopa, "Listen..."

The two boys stood very still and leaned their heads towards where the voices were coming from. It was definitely Smudge and at least two other boys.

They could hear a few words and lots of laughing, but it was the *words* that the boys found most interesting. They couldn't hear much, but they definitely heard them say 'Kolo', 'cashbox', and 'keys' amongst the other words and all the laughing.

Kolo motioned to Shoopa to stay where he was, and slowly, he tip-toed towards where the voices were coming from. He reached the corner of the wall and stood as still as he could. He knew that Smudge and his friends were just around the other side, and if they saw him or even heard him, he was done for.

His heart was beating so fast he thought they might actually hear it, but they carried on talking. He was safe for now. He listened carefully and could hear everything as clear as if they were talking right in front of him, which I suppose they were – just with the corner of a wall to separate them.

Kolo could not believe what he was hearing, but when he thought about it, it was obvious. He had just discovered who had broken into the storeroom and how.

Humble

1. How do you think the Mighty Mangoes and the wider community felt when they learnt that Kolo was not responsible for the break-in?

2. What do you think about how Kolo reacted? How would you have reacted?

3. What do you think about the reaction of the Mighty Mango players? Did they react well?

4. What do you think about the Mighty Mangoes offering to help Mr Dough?

5. What do you think this story can tell us about gossiping and how we communicate with one another?

6. What do you think this story can tell us about forgiveness and humility?

Chapter 10

KOLO REVEALS THE TRUTH

Kolo tip-toed back to Shoopa, who was still standing perfectly still as if he was a statue.

"You'll never guess what I've just found out," he whispered. "Come on," and he ran off back to where the others were still working, with Shoopa following closely behind.

"Where have you two been?" said Mosi, looking up from under an old chair. How he had managed to get beneath was anyone's guess. "How long does it take to carry a table?"

"Listen, everyone," Kolo said, "I need to tell you something, but not here; it's too risky."

They could tell from his face and the way he spoke that it was serious. Bululu wiped some dust from his forehead, and a tiny spider that had been sitting quite comfortably in his hair quickly ran off via a dirty teapot that was lying on its side on top of an old wardrobe.

"It sounds serious," he said. "Is it bad news again?"

"Not at all. It's good news, in fact," said Kolo, "but we have to go back up to Mango Park. We've done enough for today anyway; we'll finish off here tomorrow."

Midi was given the job of telling Mr Dough they would come back tomorrow, and the others raced off up to Mango Park.

They hadn't been there long before Midi joined them.

"Mr Dough's really happy with what we've done so far," he said. "Now, Kolo, what's all this about?"

Kolo told them all how he and Shoopa had heard the voices when they had gone to dump the old table and how he had gone to investigate.

"You were taking a risk," said Hami, "Smudge and his friends wouldn't have been happy if they'd seen you..."

"I know, but listen..."

Kolo then told them about what he had heard. Smudge had been bragging to his friends about how it was *him* who had got into the storeroom and stolen the money! He was laughing about how everyone thought it was Kolo and how the Mighty Mangoes were falling apart!

He obviously hadn't been at the meeting or heard about Kolo being innocent. "But how did he do it?" asked Bululu. "How did he have a key?"

"Well, do you remember the game we played against them when all their annoying little brothers came around? And do you remember that two of Smudge's brothers were teasing Coach Kato and making him chase after them?" The boys nodded.

Dave Caswell

"Well, it was all a plan," Kolo continued. "While Coach Kato was chasing them, another of one of Smudges brothers, I think they call him Sniffa, opened up the kit bag and took out the key to the storeroom. There were so many people around, especially children, no one even noticed."

"Yes!" said Midi, "I had been sent off by then and was watching the match from one of the mango trees. I saw Sniffa running as if he was being chased by a lion, and I thought it was odd because there was no one behind him. Then about ten minutes later, he came running back past the tree just as fast. I didn't think much of it at the time. Children can do all sorts of funny things, can't they? Hami used to put his shorts on his head when we were young!"

They all laughed, even Hami.

"Well, guess where Sniffa went when he was running like he was being chased by a lion?" said Kolo.

"That's it!" said Mosi, finally working things out. "His dad is the shoe repairman and also has a special machine for cutting new keys!"

"Yes, exactly!" said Kolo. He picked the story up again and continuing to tell them what he'd heard.

"According to what Smudge was saying, Sniffa had run to the shop, got a new key cut, and then came back, putting Coach Kato's key back in the kit bag and keeping the new one. That night, Smudge and his gang went to the storeroom, simply opened the door and took what they wanted. They would have taken everything, Smudge had said, but they didn't have enough arms to carry it all, and once they found the cashbox, they just left – making sure, of course, to lock the padlock behind them so one of the Mighty Mangoes would get the blame."

"That sneaky little...." Midi started to say but thankfully was interrupted.

"Now, now, Midi," said Bululu. "Remember to control your anger. You know what happened last time." Bululu was right, and Midi cooled down. He knew only too well that getting angry never ended well.

"But what do we do now? We have to do something. We know it was him!" he said.

"Yes, but he'll just deny it," said Kolo. "We'll have to come up with a plan, but for now, let's keep this to ourselves. If Smudge knows that we know, we'll never get him to confess."

The boys agreed. They needed to think things through, and they also had other important things to concentrate on, like their semi-final match against the Power Pack Pineapples.

The boys agreed with Mr Dough to have some time off from clearing the bakery storeroom so they could concentrate on training for the big match. Mr Dough was a very good man and appreciated all the hard work the boys had already done.

"Of course, boys," he said, "that old place can wait, and we want to win the match if we can. You know, I've never really liked pineapples that much anyway. Far too sweet for my taste!"

All the boys laughed.

"We'll do our very best, Mr Dough," Kolo assured him.

It was not long before the big day arrived, and the team were again playing at their home ground, Mango Park. There had been lots of rain where the Power Pack Pineapples usually played their matches, and their pitch was so full of water it was impossible to play football on. Unless, of course, you were a duck, and no one had ever seen a duck playing football.

The Power Pack Pineapples were a good team, though, and their coach, like Coach Kato, had taught them to be well behaved and respectful to others. They were nothing like the Bang Bang Bananas, and they had happily agreed to play the match at Mango Park.

The Bang Bang Bananas, incidentally, were playing in the other semi-final against the Jackfruit Juniors.

When both teams were warming up for the match, one of the Power Pack Pineapples came over to Kolo. Lots of the players knew each other, and many of them went to the same school. The boy who came over to Kolo was called Enzi and was in his class.

"Hey, Kolo," he said as he ran over, "I haven't had a chance to talk to you yet, but I'm really sorry about being unkind about your new boots and the rumours about how you'd got them. I was one of those who shared all those stories without even knowing the real truth. You know what it's like here; no one likes a thief. People have so little anyway; it's so bad when someone steals something. But I was one of those who said things, and I'm really sorry."

"That's okay," said Kolo. "It's all forgotten now. Don't worry about it."

Kolo knew how it felt to be forgiven for something and that it was the right thing to do, especially if they were truly sorry for what they had done. Enzi felt a weight lift off him. He had felt so bad before but now felt very relieved that Kolo had forgiven him.

"Thanks, Kolo," he said, "If there's anything I can do to make it up to you, just let me know."

"I will, thanks Enzi," he said, "and may the best team win!" he shouted after Enzi as he ran back to his half, leaving Kolo to continue his stretches.

"WE will!" Enzi shouted back, and both boys laughed.

The game itself was a classic; both teams played good football, and there wasn't any of the behaviour from either team that had taken place in the Mighty Mangoes game against the Bang Bang Bananas. It was played in a great spirit and with good sportsmanship, like when Shoopa slipped over when trying to go around the goalkeeper and immediately told the referee it wasn't a penalty and that he had just slipped. Not all players would have done that Kolo had thought, but the Mighty Mangoes were fair and didn't want to win by cheating.

The Power Pack Pineapples had taken an early lead with a shot that took an unfortunate deflection off Mufupi's backside as he tried to block a shot and had left Nakati in the Mangoes goal without a chance.

The Mighty Mangoes equalised with another header from 'Giraffe' – his third of the tournament - and had then gone ahead when Kolo had crossed the ball from the right for Bululu to run onto and volley into the net without even breaking his stride.

In the second half, the Pineapples brought the game level with a stunning overhead kick that even the Mangoes supporters had to applaud. But then, with 5 minutes remaining, 'Giraffe' had popped up again (quite literally) to head in the winner for the Mangoes, who would now meet either the Jackfruit Juniors or the Bang Bang Bananas in the final.

After the match, one of the Power Pack Pineapple players had joked that 'Giraffe' should play by crawling on his knees next time just to make it easier for them, but the boys knew that they would soon be catching up with him in terms of height. They were all growing taller every day.

As the two teams were shaking hands, Kolo went over to Enzi. Something had come into his mind before the match when Enzi had asked him if there was anything he could do for him.

"Hey Enzi, good game," Kolo said.

"Yeah, thanks, you too. I guess the best team didn't win after all," he joked.

"Listen," said Kolo, "Remember before the match when you asked if there was anything you could do for me? Well, I think there just might be something. You live by Smudge, don't you?"

"Yes, right next door," said Enzi, "but I wish we didn't! He and his brothers are always causing trouble. I'm sure one of them stole my football socks while they were drying on the avocado tree behind our house."

"Well, you might just be able to help us with something that will bring Smudge to justice!"

"Yes! Of course," said Enzi, "What do you want me to do?"

TEAM TALK

Forgiving

1. What was your favourite part of the story, and why?

2. Was it right for Kolo and Shoopa to listen to Smudge talking with his friends?

3. How did you feel when you learnt who had broken into the storehouse?

4. What did you think about how Kolo forgave Enzi and how Enzi had asked for forgiveness?

5. Could you ask for forgiveness, or forgive someone so easily?

6. What do you think will happen next?

Chapter 11

KOLO AND THE SMILING MANGO

Kolo met with Enzi later that evening by the large mango tree. "What I'm going to tell you is top secret," he said.

"What is it?" Enzi replied, intrigued. "I won't tell anyone, I promise."

Kolo then shared with Enzi about how Smudge had been the one responsible for the break-in and for stealing the money and the other things.

"Of course, it was him!" Enzi said when Kolo had finished. "But what do you want me to do?"

Kolo then shared with him his plan, which he had already shared with the Mighty Mangoes. All they needed was for Enzi to play his part:

"We want to set Smudge up," he began. "We want to get him to go back to the storeroom to steal something again and then catch him red-handed. He will get suspicious if any of us go around by his place, but because you live there, you can help us without him realising."

"So, what do you want me to do?" asked Enzi. He was a bit nervous as he knew Smudge was bigger than him and certainly not someone to mess with, but he also wanted to do the right thing and help Kolo.

"All we want you to do is just to talk with your friends. But say certain things and make sure that Smudge can hear them. We'll do the rest," said Kolo.

Enzi agreed, so Kolo shared what he needed to say and the two rehearsed.

"You have to do it tomorrow evening, though, and make sure Smudge hears you," Kolo said.

"I'll do my best," said Enzi. "Let's hope it works."

Kolo walked home. He hoped the plan would work. Enzi was going to do his part, and his teammates in the Mighty Mangoes were also busy organising their part of the plan. It was going to be a full 24 hours before the plan was put into action, but he knew that it would soon come around. They all just had to be patient and wait.

Kolo sat with Old Man Wilbur for a while that evening before he went to bed. They chatted about the match with the Power Pack Pineapples and how it was so much friendlier than when they had played the Bang Bang Bananas.

"Oh yes, I'm sure," said Old Man Wilbur. "I know the coach of the Pineapples, and he is a very good man. He has built up those boys to believe in themselves. They're not the best players but have very high self-esteem, and that took them a long way in the tournament."

"Self-esteem?" Kolo said. He had never heard about

that before. "What's that? Does it make them go faster, like steam on a train?"

Old Man Wilbur laughed. "Oh no, Kolo, *esteem* NOT steam, but I guess in some ways it does make you go faster! Esteem is about how you feel about yourself; generally, if you're positive and confident about yourself, you have high self-esteem, and if you feel negative or you don't have confidence, your self-esteem is lower."

"Ah, so how do I get it?" asked Kolo, still not fully understanding.

"It's not really something you get Kolo, it's more something you are, but the way people talk to you and behave towards you can affect it," said Old Man Wilbur. He really was very wise.

"There's a boy on that team, the Power Pack Pineapples. When he was younger, his father was not a very good man. He eventually left, and to be honest, that has been the best thing for him, but while he was around, he always told this boy he was 'nothing' and 'would amount to nothing' and 'would do nothing with his life.' I don't know why he was so mean; there are always reasons why people are like they are, and maybe he had his own problems, but that boy had such low self-esteem because of it. He felt bad about himself and actually believed he *was* nothing. He used to walk around with his shoulders and head so low you could think someone was pulling them down with an invisible rope!

Then he joined the Power Pack Pineapples, and the coach did a wonderful job; he used to praise him up and say good things to him and tell him how good he was at certain

107

things and that he could be anything he wanted. It took time, but eventually, he began to grow more and more in confidence and now you couldn't imagine it's the same boy. He's a good player in that team, and I hear he's doing very good at school too."

"That's amazing," said Kolo. "I also feel bad about myself when people criticise me and say bad things, and I've had my share of that lately!"

"Yes, and it can affect how you are with others too!' said Old Man Wilbur. "But yes, he's a changed thing that boy. I think he's called Enzi."

Wow! Kolo thought; Enzi was so confident and friendly, he could not imagine the transformation that had taken place. He just hoped now that his 'steam', or whatever it was called, would help him with his part of the plan.

The next day, and then the evening, came fast, and all the Mighty Mangoes were ready and in place for the plan.

Enzi took a deep breath and went out to the back of his house, where his brother was sitting. He had needed him to be involved in the plan, and they had organised things earlier. He also knew that Smudge and his friends would be there; they were always there, smashing things up and making fun of anyone who passed by.

"Hey, guess what?" Enzi said to his brother, as loud as he could but not too loud that it didn't seem obvious. "Those Mighty Mangoes are so stupid. I've just heard them talking, and they've put more money back in that storeroom of theirs, and they haven't even changed the padlock! I think they are moving the money tomorrow and changing the padlock then, but if the thieves who stole the money before knew, they could just go in again and get some more! I can't believe how stupid some people can be, can you?"

"No," said his brother, "but no one is likely to go tonight, and tomorrow the money will be taken somewhere else, the bank probably, so they'll be okay, I suppose."

Enzi and his brother couldn't be sure if Smudge had heard or not, but the group had certainly become quieter while they were talking, and then when they had started talking about something else, Smudge and his gang had disappeared pretty quickly.

Enzi at least had done his part. It was now up to Kolo and the Mighty Mangoes.

Just after dark, Smudge and his two friends made their way through the bushes and trees towards the Mighty Mangoes storeroom. They stayed off the pathways to avoid being seen and crouched down whenever they heard someone pass. At one point, Smudge had leapt up and made a strange noise that sounded like a hen being strangled, which made the other two leap up in a similar way.

"Snake!" Smudge had shouted, before flashing his small torch on the ground to reveal nothing more than an old belt.

His friends laughed, which earned them both a punch on the arm, and stopped the laughing instantly.

"Shhh, someone will hear us," Smudge said, despite the fact he had been the one making the most noise. Amazingly no one had heard or seen them.

They eventually reached the Mighty Mangoes storeroom and quickly looked around to see if anyone was about. Their eyesight was used to the dark so they could see well, but they also used the torch to make extra sure.

Smudge took the key out of his pocket and grabbed the padlock.

"Now, let's see what else these rotten mangoes have left for us," he said.

He put the key in the lock and turned it. It opened instantly, and they were in.

Smudge shone the torch around, looking for what was there. This time he had brought an old rice sack with him so they could take as much as they wanted.

"You two fill the sack," he said, "I'm looking for the money."

With that, he began to move through the storeroom and before long, he found the cash box. They had obviously bought a new one, he thought.

He picked it up and held it aloft like a trophy.

"Yes! And the winner is... *once again*... Smudge..." he whispered to his friends. "And this time, it's not even locked. How stupid are these useless mangoes?"

He opened the cashbox as his two friends, who had pretty much filled the old rice sack by now, gathered around him. As Smudge opened the box, his face dropped. There was no money in it at all, but instead, staring back at him, was a huge mango with two eyes and a massive smile carved into its skin.

"What's this!?" he cried, "Some sort of stupid joke!!!" And he punched each of his friends in their arms again, just because. How they even remained friends with him was one of life's mysteries.

Then out of the corner of his eye, he saw something move, just under one of the tables. At first, he thought it was a rat, but it was far too big to be a rat, and as far as he knew, rats didn't wear shorts and t-shirts.

"Come out!!!!" he yelled. He was really mad now and had forgotten they were supposed to be being quiet. If he hated one thing, and actually Smudge hated many things, he hated been made a fool of.

"Come out!!!!" he shouted again, "and let me bash you in – just so this entire visit isn't completely wasted."

Out from under the table came Mufupi. He was holding a small brush but how that was going to protect him from Smudge and his friends was anybody's guess.

"You've been caught, Smudge," said Mufupi. "You may as well give up."

"Caught doing what? And anyway, what can you do, especially when I've bashed you up?"

"You've been caught trying to steal from us again – just like last time when Kolo got blamed."

"Ha, ha," mocked Smudge. "Yes, of course, it was me who stole the key and got in here last time, but you're all too stupid to have caught me. Thanks for all the money, by the way."

"Is that a confession then?" said Mufupi.

"Yes! I confess to it all," laughed Smudge, "but it's my word against yours, and I'll just deny it. Who else will ever know?" He then moved towards Mufupi but was stopped in his tracks.

"*I* know," came a voice from behind him. It was Coach Kato.

"Me too," came another voice, this time belonging to Mr Dough.

"And us," shouted the rest of the Mighty Mangoes team, who were all standing at the doorway to the storeroom.

Smudge looked completely shocked. And then almost collapsed when another voice spoke. It was Mufupi's father, the policeman.

"I know too, and you are all under arrest!" he said.

Mufupi's father took all three of them straight to the police station, where they spent the night in a police cell. The next morning, when they were interviewed, they all blamed each other at first but ultimately confessed to everything.

Mufupi's father called their parents, who were, of course, very ashamed at how their boys had behaved, and promised they'd deal with them when they got home. There would be extra work in the gardens and at home, and, of course, the money would be paid back to Mr Dough and the Mighty Mangoes. In addition, Smudge was banned from playing for the Bang Bang Bananas for a whole year, starting immediately.

Smudge also confessed to other crimes he had committed and handed over a huge hoard of things he'd previously stolen, including football shorts, a pair of football boots, and Enzi's socks.

The Mighty Mangoes had not only solved the crime but had also brought those responsible to justice. It had all been Kolo's plan, but the team had carried it out to perfection, and Enzi had also played his part.

They had got the money back and could now continue in the tournament where they would play the Jackfruit Juniors in the final. The Jackfruit Juniors had beaten the Bang Bang Bananas 3-2 in the semi-final, and the Mighty Mangoes were all glad they didn't have to face them again.

Kolo, of course, was as thrilled as anyone but couldn't help feeling at least a little bit sorry for Smudge, despite all the things he had done.

Over the last few weeks, Kolo had learnt a lot; he had made mistakes himself, done things that he knew were wrong and had let people down from time to time. He had the good fortune of having people like his mother, Coach Kato and Old Man Wilbur to help him and guide him, and of course, all his friends in the Mighty Mangoes. He wondered if Smudge had anyone like that, and if he did, maybe he wouldn't be such a bully and a thug? Who knows, he thought.

Self Esteem

1. What did you like best about the story?

2. Which character did you relate to the best, and why?

3. What did you think about what Old Man Wilbur shared about self-esteem? Have you ever experienced what he talked about?

4. Who do you think did the best job in the plan to catch Smudge, and why?

5. Do you think Kolo was right to feel a bit sorry for Smudge?

6. What do you think will happen in the final?

Chapter 12

KOLO AND THE BIG MATCH

The next few weeks were good for the Mighty Mangoes. They had got the stolen money back and were now looking forward to playing in the cup final.

The boys had also finished clearing out Mr Dough's storeroom, which had been very hard work but also good training for the big match.

"I could carry the whole team after all this lifting," Mufupi said as they were completing the work and immediately wished he hadn't! The entire team took him at his word and tried to climb on top of him.

"Come on, Mufi!" - "Come on, strong man!" - "Just one more!" - they shouted as Mufupi tried his best to hold them all, with player after player added themselves to some part of his body.

"No problem," he shouted through clenched teeth, trying to stay upright until eventually, it was just too much, and they all collapsed in a heap laughing once again until their cheeks were sore.

While clearing out the storeroom, Kolo had come across a photograph of a football team, clearly from a very long time ago. The picture was in black and white and was curled up at either end, rather like a slice of watermelon. The boys had taken great interest in the photo when Kolo had shown it to them.

"Maybe this is The Mighty Mangoes from years ago?" Midi had suggested.

"Maybe," said Hami, "we should ask Mr Dough."

They took the photo to Mr Dough, but he didn't know who was in it or where it had come from.

"I have no idea, boys," he said. "As you'll know, there were all sorts of things in that storeroom, but you can keep it if you like."

Kolo put the photograph in his pocket and promised to take good care of it. He, of course, loved football, and this photo would join the collection of pictures he had gathered over the years.

Time went quickly, and with the final just a few days away, the boys were training hard. They were extremely committed and knew they needed to train well if they were to beat the Jackfruit Juniors, who were arguably the best team in the region.

It was the first time the Mighty Mangoes had ever reached the final, and there was a lot of excitement in the community; posters had been put up on trees and electricity poles advertising the match, and Mr Dough had produced some special mango-flavoured buns in tribute to the Mighty Mangoes.

The training was good; Coach Kato was helping them focus on their passing and movement (things he said were crucial in football) and also on their fitness. He had told the players that one or two of them looked like they had eaten a few too many of Mr Doughs mango buns!

It was during one of the last training sessions just days before the final that disaster struck. Bululu was running for the ball and, seemingly without reason, just collapsed on the floor. All the boys immediately ran over to him.

"My ankle!" Bululu cried. "It's my ankle!"

They looked down, and already his ankle was starting to swell up. Bululu had stepped in a hole as he was running for the ball and had twisted his ankle badly.

"Let's get you to the clinic," Coach Kato said, and the Mighty Mangoes (including Mufupi, who of course 'could carry the whole team') carried their captain to the nearby clinic.

Dr Bonemenda checked out the injury and said it was a good sign that Bululu could 'wiggle his toes.'

"It's a nasty twist, though," he said. "But you'll be okay in a week or two. You just need to rest it. I'll give you some painkillers and strap it up with a bandage."

"But what about the match?" Bululu said.

"Oh, I'm sorry, young man," said Dr Bonemenda. "There's no way you can play football for at least two weeks."

Bululu was devastated; he was in a lot of pain but felt

117

much worse in the pit of his stomach. It was as if someone had punched him and knocked all of the air out of him.

He tried to hold in the tears (he wanted to be tough in front of his friends), but it was just too hard. Two big tears started to roll down his cheeks, closely followed by what can only be described as a waterfall. He thought his friends would laugh, which would make it even worse, but instead, they comforted him. He was their friend and their team captain, and all of them, every single one, could understand. They would feel exactly the same if it was them.

One by one, they did their bit to make him feel better. Some put their arms around him or patted him on the back, while others offered words of comfort:

"Don't worry, Bululu, you helped get us to the final. You have played your part."

"We wouldn't even be there if it wasn't for you."

"We'll win it for you, Bululu!"

"Be strong, even Messi gets injured sometimes, and he's nowhere near as good as you!"

The last comment raised a slight smile from Bululu.

"Thanks, boys," he said. "I've never known friends like you before."

"We're the Mighty Mangoes!!!" Hami exclaimed. "We're together through good and bad. And always there for each other. Always!"

The boys cheered, Bululu smiled again, and some of the other nurses and doctors at the clinic came and looked into the room, which was packed with the Mighty Mangoes.

"And now, we have to do one more thing... but very, very carefully..." Kolo said.

"MANGO CRUSH!!!"

All the boys hugged Bululu as the doctors and nurses looked on and laughed.

"You have good friends there," said one of them to Bululu, who was somewhere in the middle of it all with his injured ankle sticking out at one side. It looked like a very funny sight.

"Where's Dr Bonemenda?" one of the nurses suddenly asked. "He was here a minute ago!"

"I'm here!" came a voice from the heart of the Mango Crush. "I think I've just experienced my first ever Mango Crush!!!"

It was a big blow for the Mighty Mangoes to be without their captain for the final, especially against the Jackfruit Juniors, who had won the cup the year before, but who would replace Bululu?

Coach Kato gathered the boys together after their last training session before the big match. Although he couldn't train, Bululu was also there; being with the rest of the team was good for him – and for the team.

"With Bululu out, we need to appoint a new captain for the match tomorrow," said Coach Kato. "Now I have my own thoughts, but what do you think?"

The boys thought for only a second or two and then exploded into noisy chatting, which Kolo thought sounded quite like the noise a group of chickens make when a snake turns up!

Various names were suggested, debated, dismissed – and then suggested, debated, and dismissed again!

Several boys suggested Hami – he was well disciplined, inspirational and was well respected by the team.

Equally, Mufupi had similar qualities.

Another person suggested 'Giraffe' as in their words he was, 'head and shoulders above everyone else,' and everybody groaned.

Kolo was also suggested by a number of the boys.

"Thanks, but I can't be captain," Kolo said. "I've only just joined the team, and others can do a much better job than me."

"Yeah, but you're a good leader Kolo," Shoopa said. "Remember how it was you who made the plan to catch Smudge, and we all went along with it? You led us well."

"Maybe," said Kolo, a little embarrassed, "but that wasn't just me; we all contributed. Any one of us could be captain. What's important is that we all play our part and respect whoever it is, which I know we'll do."

Coach Kato then spoke, "Kolo is right; any one of you could be captain, so this is what we're going to do. I'm going to give you bits of paper, and I want you to write the name of the person you would like to be captain. Then fold it in half and put it in this cap that I'm going to pass round." And with that, he grabbed Mosi's cap off his head and held it in the air.

Coach Kato passed the papers and some pencils around, and the boys wrote down their choice for captain. When they'd finished, the papers had been collected, and Mosi's cap had been returned to his head, Coach Kato announced the result.

"The captain for tomorrow's match is... wait for it... any second now... I'm about to announce it..."

"Come on, Coach!!!!" the Mighty Mangoes shouted."

"The captain is... Kolo!"

The Mighty Mangoes cheered, slapped him on the back, and began shouting "Kolo, Kolo, Kolo..." as they danced around him.

"It's a big responsibility, Kolo," said Coach Kato, "But you can do it, and do you know what, your teammates believe in you. Every single person voted for you."

Kolo smiled a mango slice smile.

"Thank you," he said, "I'll do my very best."

He had never felt prouder and so loved (except by his mother, of course, but that goes without saying). He felt tears building up in his eyes, and just like Bululu earlier, a couple of tears ran down each cheek - before the waterfall followed.

He knew what was coming and braced himself for a 'Mango Crush!'

Walking home after training, Kolo reflected on the events of the last few days, and especially how he and Bululu had both cried at different times and for very different reasons

– and how the Mighty Mangoes were there for them and didn't seem to mind. He knew lots of boys would make fun of someone for crying, but not the Mighty Mangoes.

Reaching home, he saw that his mother had done some washing, which in itself wasn't unusual but, hanging on the rope she used to put the washing out to dry, was what looked like a piece of paper or card.

"My photo!" yelled Kolo, running over.

"Oh yes, I wondered who's that was. It almost got a good scrubbing when I was washing your shorts, but thankfully it's just had a little bath instead," his mother said. "It's fine, just a little damp."

Kolo ran over to inspect the photo, and indeed it was 'fine.' In fact, it was quite dry now and even looked a bit better than before.

Kolo could hear laughing behind him and knew where it was coming from.

"Oh, Kolo," shouted Old Man Wilbur, "washing photographs now? Whatever next!"

Kolo laughed himself and took the photo over to show Old Man Wilbur, who, as always, was sitting on his stool outside his house.

"I found it in Mr Dough's storehouse," he said, "I wonder if you know who the people in it are?"

"Oh my, oh my!" exclaimed Old Man Wilbur, "I do indeed, Kolo, I do indeed! That is the Amazing Avocados Football Club, and that there at the end of the back row is me! This is my old team!"

Kolo was himself amazed, although he wasn't an avocado. He couldn't imagine Old Man Wilbur off his stool, let alone playing football.

"Oh yes, Kolo, I was quite a player in my day. I used to play on the left-wing, and I was as fast as a cheetah. We had a good team in those days, just like you have now."

They talked into the evening about football, and Old Man Wilbur shared lots of stories of his time with the Amazing Avocados and other stories about when he was a child. Kolo loved hearing the old stories, and he knew that Old Man Wilbur loved sharing them too. He wondered how many other old men, or old women for that matter, had things to share but no one to share them with. Kolo felt blessed for knowing Old Man Wilbur, and he suspected Old Man Wilbur felt the same.

That night, Kolo hardly slept. It was the cup final tomorrow, and not only that, but he was also to be the captain of the Mighty Mangoes. His stomach was full of a mixture of excitement and nervousness, and of course, the rice and beans that they had had for supper.

The next day, Kolo and the Mighty Mangoes arrived at The Fruit Bowl Stadium for the big match. The Jackfruit Juniors were already there, warming up and taking in the atmosphere which was building by the minute. Most of the other teams were also there to watch; the Awesome Apples, the Guava Giants, and the Power Pack Pineapples, to name just a few. There were even a few of the Bang Bang Bananas there.

There were plenty of supporters of the Mighty Mangoes too. It looked to Kolo like the entire village had turned up to watch. Most of the boys' parents, grandparents and brothers and sisters were there; Mr Dough was there wearing a very smart shirt with pictures of cakes on it, and a number of his staff were also there selling lots of the special edition mango buns!

Mr Dough could not allow all his staff to be away from the bakery, but a number were there, and Kolo's mother, of course, had been given permission to attend. She was sitting with Kolo's sister, the man with the wobbly bicycle and his wife with the big curly hair, and... No! It couldn't be! Kolo had to rub his eyes just to make sure he was seeing properly. It was Old Man Wilbur!

"Go on, Kolo!" shouted Old Man Wilbur, waving his walking stick about just a bit too much that he knocked the hat clean off the head of the man in front of him.

"Oh, I'm so sorry!" he said. "I'm just terribly excited."

"No problem," the man in front replied, bending to retrieve his hat, "I'm terribly excited myself; my two boys are playing today, Midi and Hami."

"Oh, that's brilliant," said Old Man Wilbur. "I'm a neighbour of Kolo, and I know you have two good boys there."

"Thank you," the man said, "Kolo is a good boy too; he's been a great friend to them."

The two men continued to talk as the build-up to the match went on, and more and more people made their way into the stadium.

In the dressing room, Coach Kato gave the Mighty Mangoes an inspiring team talk, and then, as captain for the day, it was Kolo's turn to say something:

"These last few months have been great for me. There have been some really difficult times, but mostly really good times. I've never known a team like the Mighty Mangoes; you're all kind and caring, and true, true friends with one another... (At this point, he felt he might cry again but managed to compose himself.) We are one team, we are one family, we are the Mighty Mangoes! Now, let's go out there and win this match for every one of us, for all our parents and supporters, for Coach Kato, and especially for our great captain, Bululu!" (At which point Bululu felt like *he* might cry!)

The boys cheered and shouted, and Kolo felt a 'Mango Crush' might be on its way, but at that point, the referee poked his head around the door.

"Come on, boys, we're ready to go," he said.

The Mighty Mangoes moved out into the tunnel where they stood next to the Jackfruit Juniors, waiting for further instructions from the referee. Once they were all there, the referee indicated for the teams to move out, and Kolo, full of pride, led the Mighty Mangoes out onto the pitch to a massive roar from the crowd.

Kolo was extremely nervous as the game started (as, understandably, were most of the boys), but once things got going, he relaxed a bit more and started to enjoy the occasion. His first few passes were good, and he also had a shot in the opening 10 minutes that only just missed the top corner.

125

It was a tough game, and the Mighty Mangoes had to be at their best, even just to match the Jackfruit Juniors. They had better players and were obvious favourites to win the game. However, if the Mighty Mangoes lacked a little in terms of ability, they had more than enough commitment and determination to compensate.

The game was fairly evenly matched; the first half was tight, with few chances for either side. The Jackfruit Juniors probably had the best opportunity when their star striker was clean through after Mufupi slipped trying to clear the ball, but the Mighty Mangoes 'keeper, Nakati, made a stunning save to his left to tip the ball around the post. The Jackfruit Juniors had other chances, but great defending from the Mighty Mangoes had kept them out.

At the other end, apart from Kolo's shot early on that just missed, 'Giraffe' headed just over, and Shoopa hit a rocket of a shot that rattled the crossbar – to the disappointment of all the Mighty Mangoes supporters.

The first half ended with the referee's whistle and the scores level at 0-0.

In the dressing room, Coach Kato was pleased with the team's performance, especially defensively, but encouraged them to be a little braver in the second half and, in his words, 'Put the Jackfruits Juniors on the backfoot.'

Kolo also gave another encouraging team talk and then invited Bululu, who, of course, was with them all, to say a few words too.

"Kolo has done a great job as captain," Bululu began, to nods of agreement from the boys. "He is a great leader, but actually, you are all captains, you are all leaders; it is not Kolo's job to win this match, and it isn't mine. It is for all of us to win it. We are all captains; we are all leaders; we are all one giant mighty mango!"

The last bit made them laugh, but they were equally inspired.

"Let's do this!" shouted Shoopa, and the boys went out for the second half, believing they could beat anyone.

The second half was more open than the first, with both sides having chances and the Mighty Mangoes pushing forward a little more to try and press the Jackfruits. This approach paid off for the Mangoes halfway through the half when Shoopa superbly controlled a ball from Mosi on his chest before laying it off to Kolo, who hit it first time and into the back of the net from the edge of the penalty area. The goalkeeper hardly saw it!

The Mighty Mangoes supporters went wild with celebrations! Kolo ran to the corner flag with the rest of the team, apart from the goalkeeper, Nakati, who was doing a handstand in his penalty box, running to meet and embrace him. What a goal! What a moment!

Once things had settled down and the game restarted, the Jackfruit Juniors came at the Mighty Mangoes with full force. It was as if they'd poked a sleeping lion with a stick! They threw everything at them, but the Mighty Mangoes blocked every chance that came their way; Mufupi took a shot full in the face and needed a bit of treatment for a cut above his eye, and Mosi also needed treatment for a kick on his ankle. The Jackfruit Juniors hit both the post and the crossbar, and Midi cleared another shot off the line.

127

It looked like it was going to be the Mighty Mangoes day, and the Jackfruit Juniors wouldn't score if they played all night – and the whole of the next day - but with 5 minutes remaining, they got the goal, which, to be honest, they had deserved. Nakati made another spectacular save, but the ball rebounded out to the Jackfruits striker, who, with Nakati stranded, blasted it into the empty net.

The Mighty Mangoes were devastated. They had given everything and could barely walk, let alone run.

"Come on," said Kolo, "we can still do this. Don't give up! The Mighty Mangoes never give up!"

Others, whose heads had been so low moments before you could have been mistaken for thinking they were attached to their chests, joined in with the call to 'go again'.

"Yes, come on, boys, it's not over."

"One last effort."

"We can do it!"

And then... "Let's do it for Bululu!"

Every one of the Mighty Mangoes raised their heads, put their shoulders back, and went for the win.

The Jackfruit Juniors were stunned by the response from the Mighty Mangoes; there were only 3 minutes left, but the Mangoes seemed to have got some extra energy from somewhere – and not only energy but confidence. They ran to find space for each other, to get the ball back when they had lost it, and to get in a position to have a goal attempt.

With time running out and looking like the game would go to extra time, Kolo received a ball from Mosi on the left-hand side. He took it past one player, through the legs of another and bore down on goal. This was it. This was the moment. His legs were heavy, but he kept on going. He drew his leg back to shoot and had made his mind up where he was aiming, but just as he was about to kick the ball, he found himself going backwards. The Jackfruit Juniors defender had grabbed his shirt and was pulling him backwards; he swiped at the ball the best he could but missed it completely and fell flat on his back.

From his position down on the pitch, he turned his head to look at the referee, as too did all the players from both sides - and all the supporters.

It seemed to take forever as the referee ran over. He lifted his arm and pointed to the penalty spot.

PENALTY to the Mighty Mangoes.

Bululu was the normal penalty taker, but with him not involved on the pitch, it had to be up to someone else.

"I don't mind taking it," said Kolo, as the players gathered together, "I'm the captain after all, and I'll take the responsibility if no one else wants to take it, but I'd like to give someone else the chance. Hami, would you like to take it?"

Hami looked at him.

"But I've never taken a penalty in my life, not in a proper game at least," he said, "What if I miss?"

"If you miss, you miss," said Kolo, "no problem, we're still together." Everyone looked at Kolo and then looked at Hami.

"Listen, Hami," said Kolo, "I don't want you to feel any pressure, and I'll take the penalty if everyone agrees, but you've been a great player for the Mighty Mangoes, and more than that, you're a great person. It's about time you got some recognition."

"If you're sure?" said Hami. "I'd love to take it."

All the players agreed, and Hami picked up the ball and placed it on the penalty spot.

In the crowd, someone not far from Hami's father and clearly a Jackfruit Juniors supporter made a rather unpleasant comment:

"Ha! Surely, *he's* not going to take it! He's only got one arm!!!" He said, and a few people around him laughed.

Hami's father turned towards where the voice had come from:

"Listen here," he shouted, "first of all, you don't take penalties with your arms; you take them with your feet - and he's got two of those! And secondly, he may only have one arm, but he has the heart of a lion and is more of a man than you will ever be! Now be quiet and have some respect!"

Everyone around them cheered and clapped, and the man felt as small as a mosquito.

Hami took a long walk away from the ball and then turned to wait for the referee's whistle. The ref blew the whistle, and Hami took a deep breath. He ran towards the ball and hit it as cleanly as he had ever hit a football. The goalkeeper was nowhere near it, and it flew into the bottom corner of the net.

130

GOAL!!!!!!!

What followed can only be described as unbelievable scenes of celebration, both on the pitch and off it.

In the crowd, Hami's father took his hat off and threw it in the air, Old Man Wilbur leapt from his seat and would have ended up on the floor if Kolo's mother hadn't grabbed hold of him and hugged him, and the man with the wobbly bicycle and his wife with the big curly hair embraced each other. Mr Dough danced with his bakery staff, and Dr Bonemenda, who just had to come and watch after having experienced his first Mango Crush at the clinic, lifted his arms in triumph.

The minute left of the match seemed like an hour to the Mighty Mango players, but when the referee blew the final whistle, more celebrations ensued, despite the fact the celebrations after the penalty had barely come to an end. It was more like a continuation.

The Mighty Mangoes embraced each other before commiserating with the Jackfruit Juniors, who, themselves, had played a good game and wished them well.

After things had died down a little, the time came to lift the trophy. And the 'captain' of the Mighty Mangoes was called on the loudspeaker to step forward.

"They're calling you, Bululu," Kolo said.

"But you were the captain today Kolo," Bululu replied, "They're calling *you*."

"I was only standing in for you," Kolo said.

"I tell you what, let's go together," said Bululu, and so together, the two of them climbed the stairs.

They took the trophy from Mayor Goldchain together, and again together, they lifted it to huge cheers and applause. It seemed that 'together' could sum up the Mighty Mangoes.

The Mighty Mangoes and their supporters arrived back at Mango Park, where they were met by the entire community who had come out to congratulate them. Food had been prepared, and sodas purchased to celebrate the victory. Kolo had never seen anything like it.

They partied way into the night: dancing, singing and laughing. Even Old Man Wilbur had a little dance before returning to the wooden stool that he had brought with him to Mango Park.

During the evening, Coach Kato took Kolo to one side.

"What a day, Kolo!" he said, "I couldn't be prouder of you and the team. You see what an impact it has had on this community of ours."

"It's amazing," said Kolo, "but everyone has done something; it isn't just down to me or even the other players. You're a brilliant coach and a great mentor; you have helped me a lot. Then there's Mr Dough, and Old Man Wilbur, and many others. This team of ours is much bigger than just us players; I've realised that."

"Yes, you're right, Kolo, very right, but it also doesn't hurt to give praise to one another as individuals too. I have seen you change and grow as a person, Kolo, and it thrills my heart. You're compassionate and considerate, joyful and hopeful, patient and have good self-control; you've shown yourself to be honest and forgiving, and certainly humbler than when we first met! And on top of all that, you've shown great commitment and teamwork, built and restored lots of relationships and helped to build up the self-esteem of others. And you've shown excellent communication and leadership skills."

"Wow! You make me sound like an amazing person."

"You are. But you're amazing regardless of all that. Just by being you. All of us are amazing; we just need to keep on working on the things we struggle with and continue doing the things we're good at. And we need each other to do that," said Coach Kato. "Many years ago, when I was a boy, I was terrible, a bit like Smudge, and you know what a pain he can be."

"I can't imagine you like that!" Kolo said. "Really?"

"Yes, really," said Coach Kato, "but someone took time to talk with me and guide me. He helped me a lot, and now I want to help others in the same way; even Smudge is not beyond help, and I'm happy to have done something small in your life, too, Kolo."

"You certainly have, Coach, and I'm grateful, but who was the person who helped you when you were young?"

"Oh, that man," he said, "he was a good man, and he still is. He used to make training a lot of fun and would have a saying he would always share with us as players, especially when we were feeling down."

"What did he used to say?" Kolo asked.

"Ah, he always used to say: 'Laugh lots, and you'll live long,' and he's proven that to be true."

"Old Man Wilbur!" Kolo cried excitedly.

"Yes, Kolo, Old Man Wilbur."

Leadership

1. What was your favourite part of the story, and why?

2. How did you feel when Bululu hurt his ankle and was out of the cup final? Has anything similar happened to you?

3. What do you think about the way the Mighty Mangoes responded when Bululu was injured?

4. Do you think it was okay for both Bululu and Kolo to cry?

5. What qualities do you think make a good leader?

6. Was Kolo a good leader, and why?

7. What important qualities did you see in the Mighty Mangoes team during the story?

8. Do you have any thoughts about the conversation Coach Kato and Kolo had at the end of the story?

Kolo and the Mighty Mangoes:
EXTRA TIME

You may wish to follow up on the stories and themes of
Kolo & the Mighty Mangoes with the following discussion
questions and activity suggestions:

1. Kolo lives with his mother and sister, and his father is
   never mentioned. Why do you think this might be?

2. We never learn how Hami came to have only one
   arm. Do you have any thoughts or suggestions why he
   only has one arm?

3. Have you ever had to move to a new place and make
   new friends? How did you feel?

4. How do you treat new people who come to your
   community or school?

5. Who was your favourite character in the stories, and
   why?

6. Have you ever found yourself in any of the situations
   in the story? How did you react, and how would you
   react now?

7. If the Mighty Mangoes had lost in the final, how would you feel and react? How do you think the Mighty Mangoes would feel and react, and would it be different?

8. What are the main things you have learnt from the stories that you could apply to your life?

9. Which of the 'habits' and 'life skills' do you struggle with most?

10. What thing(s) will you do differently now?

Some suggested activities:

1. Write or tell a story about Old Man Wilbur when he was younger and playing for the Amazing Avocados.

2. Draw/make a club badge for the Mighty Mangoes.

3. Write or tell a story about what happens next for Kolo and the Mighty Mangoes.

4. Draw a picture of your favourite character. What do you think they might look like?

5. Do some action or activity in the community that the Mighty Mangoes would be proud of.

ABOUT OASIS

Oasis is a group of charities founded by Steve Chalke, set up to pioneer sustainable and holistic local community transformation models. Wherever we work, we serve and respect all people, whatever their gender, race, ethnic orientation, religion, age, sexual orientation or physical and mental capability, through the pursuit of our two global goals:

- To build and help others build strong, inclusive communities where every person can find their place, flourish and achieve their God-given potential.
- To work with those who find themselves outside of a healthy community to find their place once again.

Currently, Oasis works in 42 local neighbourhoods in England and another 26 in countries around the world. Our approach is always bespoke, tailored to each local community or group of people we work with.

Oasis has over five thousand staff, as well as many more thousands of volunteers. We are responsible for more than fifty schools, thirty thousand students, and numerous housing and health projects. Through working with local community members, we are also involved in developing everything from foodbanks to debt advice centres; savings clubs to credit unions; local churches to city farms; community shops to breakfast clubs; children's centres to refugee housing; initiatives to combat human trafficking and sexual and gender-based violence to adult numeracy and literacy courses; libraries to football teams; partnerships with the NHS to employment initiatives, and much more.

Together we are building communities where everyone can thrive.

To find out more, or to discover how to get involved or support us, please visit:

www.oasisuk.org

ABOUT OASIS FOOTBALL FOR LIFE

O asis Football for Life (FFL) is an Oasis initiative serving as a central supportive, consultative, and resourcing body for the implementation, development and monitoring of football projects across the Oasis family.

Across the world, in the communities where Oasis works, children and young people are at risk of early sexual activity, vulnerable to HIV/AIDS and other Sexually Transmitted Diseases. They often engage in drug and alcohol abuse, violence, and other anti-social behaviour. Oasis Football for Life projects work with these vulnerable and marginalised children and young people, using football as the medium for building confidence and self-esteem, and teaching valuable life skills, helping them to make healthy and informed life choices.

FFL seeks to help children and young people develop a mind-set and attitude of inclusion and community cohesion. It is intentional in engaging young people of different social, religious and ethnic backgrounds, reducing the risk of young people engaging in extremist groups, gangs, and other exclusive activity.

FFL also seeks to grow leaders and create change agents; people equipped to contribute to their own transformation, that of others, and that of their community.

ABOUT THE OASIS 9 HABITS

The Oasis 9 Habits have been created and developed by Oasis as a foundational approach for the development or formation of character. They are an invitation to a way of life characterised by being:

Humble, Hopeful, Honest, Forgiving, Patient, Joyful, Self-Controlled, Considerate, Compassionate.

Each of the 'Habits' are core attributes or character traits that express what it means to be fully human and which, once embraced and developed, can help people live life to its full potential in true community and relationship and to flourish themselves.

Like all habits, they need to be practised and grown. To support this, an extensive range of 9 Habits tools and resources have been developed by Oasis in the UK.

The Oasis 9 Habits are core to the work of Oasis, particularly in the UK, and are being used extensively in UK hubs and academies.

Football in and of itself can be a valuable medium for helping to support the social, emotional, physical, and educational development of children and young people, and there are key aspects of football that naturally lends itself to the development of the Oasis 9 Habits.

ABOUT THE AUTHOR

Dave Caswell has worked with Oasis in International Community Development since 2004. He has a Masters in Intercultural Studies, with a concentration in 'Children at Risk', and has lived and worked in Uganda, India, North America, and South Africa. He currently lives in the UK, where he works as the Global Coordinator of Oasis Football for Life, supporting the implementation, development and resourcing of 'Football for Development' projects across the global Oasis family.